Deadly Paradise

An Al Pennyback Mystery

Charles Ray

North Potomac, Maryland

This book is a work of fiction. Names, characters, places, and incidents are products of the author's imagination or are used factiously. Any resemblance to actual events or locales or persons, living or dead, is entirely coincidental.

An Original Publication of UHURU PRESS.

For information about this book, or other works by this author, contact charlesray.author@yahoo.com or check the author's website at: http://charlesaray.blogspot.com/.

Printed in the United States of America.

ISBN: 0615790747
ISBN-13: 978-0615790749 (Uhuru Press)

1.

It was the last week in June and summer already had Washington, DC by the throat, like a terrier with a rat in its jaws, and it wasn't letting go, just squeezing inexorably pressing the life out of everything, not really flinging it about exactly as a terrier would, but clamping down and holding it still, watching with gleaming eyes as it closed the breathing passages. Cruel it is; as cruel as a cat that plays with its food before finally killing and eating it.

It was Wednesday, June 21, hump day, the middle of the work week for most people. Of course, I'm not most people. I don't have a normal work week. I don't do normal work. I'm a private detective. That's a lot like being a day worker; the kind of guy who stands on a street corner waiting for a rusty pickup or moving van to come along so he can make minimum wage for eight to twelve hours of backbreaking work in the heat, and then go home to a house with no air conditioning. Okay, so maybe I make more than minimum wage, but day workers get work more often than I do, so I think it probably evens out in the end.

It was ten days before the really hot part of the summer would ordinarily be starting, but summer had gotten a jump on the calendar, and only twelve days until I turned fifty. That latter fact was bothering me almost as much as the weather. I mean, fifty is old, right? That's when strange changes are supposed to take place, and I wasn't sure I was looking forward to them, whatever they were. When I was a kid, growing up in rural East Texas, people who were fifty were *old*. They looked old, they acted old, and they *smelled* old. It was like, on the day of your fiftieth birthday, a switch in your body flipped and you became this withered, alien being who bore no resemblance to the person who'd drifted off to sleep the night before. None of my friends were fifty; in fact, of all my friends, I was the closest to that mysterious age. Would they, I wondered, treat me differently the day I 'changed?'

The temperatures by midday were already pegging out in the high nineties, with humidity hovering around eighty-nine percent. Whenever I went outside, sheets of sweat would envelop me like a scratchy old army blanket, soaking my shirt and pants, and leaving dark circles at the underarms, crotch, inner elbow, and just about anywhere else where seams came together. It would have been embarrassing if not for the fact that everyone was afflicted with the same condition. The heat was visible, undulating waves rising up from the concrete like a gauzy veil, shimmering and turning the landscape into a blurry scene like one of those paintings that look like the artist was high on something when he painted them.

Normally, June is girl watching weather. It brings out all the secretaries and sales clerks to hang about the many parks and other green spaces, wearing dresses appropriate for the warm weather; dresses that were as short as the law allowed, that covered the essentials, but not too much. Skirts that were often little more than an extension of a blouse or T-shirt, displaying the soft, desirable areas of a woman's anatomy that had been covered for months against winter's chill. But, the weather was so hot, the girls, the smart ones at least, stayed inside where air conditioners groaned as they strained vainly to keep the heat out. The ones dumb enough to come out in the heat usually didn't get a second glance – if indeed they even got the first one. There's nothing sexy about being as red as a freshly cooked lobster and sweating like a lumberjack. And, in a few years, overexposure to the sun would have their skin looking like an expanse of parched desert, if they were lucky; if not, they'd be getting treatment for carcinoma.

I didn't even bother to look out the one window in my little office. The trees, their thick green leaves looking forlorn in the shimmering heat, blocked my view of the Washington Channel and the Potomac River beyond. I could, had I chosen to look, see the light gray sides of the towering condos that stuck up through the trees like giant boxes, gleaming in the afternoon sun, or the bright blue, cloudless sky. But, as boring as I find paperwork, it was preferable to the unbroken sameness outside.

I was checking over case files that my assistant, partner, friend, Heather Bunche had typed and stacked neatly on the left rear corner of my desk. I'd had in- and outboxes once upon a time, but the mere sight of them bothered me. They made me feel like a bureaucrat, and the way I feel about bureaucrats, it just didn't seem right, so I asked Heather to get rid of them. I never found out what she did with them, but, I did notice that she removed the ones from her desk as well. The last report in the stack was the most recently finished case; an investigation into the suspicious death of an elderly resident of a nursing home in Rockville, Maryland. The case hadn't strained my ability, and had only marginally improved our bank account, but every dollar counted. The ten thousand a month retainer we got from the law firm of Holcombe, Stein and Chang covered the rent, utilities, and

Heather's salary – most months. I also had a little nest egg from my army retirement. But, if you don't have more coming in than you have going out, the law of arithmetic says you'll end up broke one day. I worry about such things.

My name, for the benefit of the curious, is Albert Einstein 'Al' Pennyback. Al to my friends, what few I have, and Mr. Pennyback to everyone else, unless they have a death wish. At six feet and just a few ounces under two hundred pounds, with only a few grams of fat around the middle now that I'm knocking hard on fifty; with black belts in taekwondo and karate, and more than a nodding acquaintance with judo and kendo, I'm no slouch when it comes to bruising people if it becomes necessary. I don't smile much, and with a broad forehead, slightly bent nose, wide set brown eyes in a face that's the color of caramel, under slightly curled hair that can't decide whether it's black or brown – and lately has been showing flecks of gray – I probably don't look like someone you want to mess with. Not, mind you, that it stops everyone. The determined or demented ones sometimes take a run at me. Them I handle.

We're quite the team, Heather and I. I started 'A.E. Pennyback, Confidential Enquiries,' right after my wife Sarah and my son Ethan were killed in an accident when the van Sarah was driving to bring Ethan and some of his team mates back into the District from an evening soccer game in Arlington was T-boned by a truck driver who ignored a stop sign as he entered Arlington Boulevard from a side street. I was in the army at the time, a lieutenant colonel on assignment at the Pentagon. When I came out of the blue funk the accident had plunged me into, I put in my retirement papers.

For a few weeks, I sat around our house in Georgetown, staring at the walls, trying to convince myself I was in a long nightmare, and would awaken to find Sarah and Ethan standing in front of me. It never happened. I blamed myself for their deaths, even though I knew there was nothing I could have done to prevent it. The human mind's funny that way, though. It finds all kinds of amazing, convoluted ways to deal with unpleasant things; denial, guilt, rage, withdrawal; I went through them all. None of it brought my family back.

Finally, Quincy Chang, a partner in the law firm Holcombe, Stein, and Chang, and an old friend from our days together at Fort Bragg, North Carolina, when he served in the judge advocate office and I was running around the world chasing after drug lords and other assorted miscreants, dragged me out of my self-imposed exile from humanity. He convinced me to use the skills I'd developed in just over twenty years in army special operations in a private capacity. Helped me get my PI license and then convinced his partners to put me on a ten thousand buck a month retainer doing odd jobs for the firm.

That was over ten years ago. They'd never bothered to offer me more, but I wasn't one to complain. All I ever had to do for them was track down the occasional lost heir to some estate or find a deadbeat client who tried to duck out on paying the fees they owed. The rest of the time I could devote to taking the occasional case that floated in over the transom. Those didn't usually pay much, but they were always interesting – and, sometimes dangerous.

It was enough to pay the rent, fees, and Heather's salary. I'd used the money Sarah and I'd been putting away for six years for Ethan's college fund and bought an old farm in Montgomery County, Maryland, along River Road just west of Potomac Village. The place hadn't been much to look at – still wasn't a whole lot to look at – but, it had become home. The old man who'd lived there for over forty years had died, and his two sons who lived in California didn't want to get stuck paying property taxes on a place they'd never live in, so they gave me a good deal. It had a wood frame house that was solidly built, and a barn that leaned a little, but, was also built when things were constructed to last, and sufficed for my uses. It was at the end of a winding dirt road that cut off River Road, winding through high grass to the house, and a hardwood and pine forest behind it that wound down to the C&O Canal and the Potomac River. If you didn't know the road was there, you'd drive right past it. I liked it like that.

During most of the year, I could stand at my kitchen sink, looking out the window, and watch small herds of deer grazing in my back yard. It was especially nice in the spring, right after the new fawns had gotten old enough to wander far afield with their moms, and were agile enough to throw up their ivory tails and bound into the woods whenever I opened the back door to get a closer look at them. Sometimes in winter, when the snow was deep enough to choke off the few shoots still clinging to the frozen ground, I'd go to the feed store up River Road not far from the I-495 Beltway, and buy several bales of hay, which I'd put out in back near the barn. People were warned against doing this because the deer were vectors for Lyme disease and they could do a number on decorative plants. But, I never got close to them, didn't roll around in the grass so I doubt I'd been exposed to the ticks that are the real carriers, and had no plants that I worried about them damaging, and, I hated to see them suffer.

I jogged through the forest most mornings, scattering birds, deer, and other forest creatures, and then worked out in the barn on a heavy bag suspended from the rafters, until I worked up a good sweat. My exercise sessions always ended with ten to twenty minutes of meditation, either on my back porch, or, if the weather was bad, inside the house.

I'd had the kitchen completely redone, with the latest appliances, and until Sandra Winter, my current girlfriend, had more or less moved in with me – she kept her little house in Takoma Park on the border between DC and Montgomery County, but spent most of her time at my – our – place – I'd been the only one to use or appreciate it.

Sandra is a teacher at Carter High School, a prison-like red brick structure in one of Washington's poorer neighborhoods, where students are as likely to carry a gun or knife to school as books. I met her when I was working on a case involving one of her students who'd been gunned down while running an errand for his grandmother, and we'd been almost inseparable since.

I continued to shuffle the papers around on my desk, but I was just kidding myself. I've never been fond of or good at doing paperwork. I'm more at home in the field or on the streets. That's why I hired Heather right out of secretarial school; so I'd be free to spend my time outside the office. But, in order to do that I needed a case to work on - and there was nothing, absolutely nothing. I was so bored I found myself sitting there listening to the hums, clinks and burps coming from the cooling system and wondering if maybe there was something in the pipes causing it or if it was just a combination of loose pipes and the force of the air moving through them. Yes, I was that bored.

Finally, I gave up, got up, and walked to the outer office, where I found Heather sitting looking at her computer screen, a faraway look on her face.

"I'm bored," she said.

"Me too," I said.

Heather is seldom bored. At least, I'd never seen her bored. She was usually pecking away at her computer keyboard, occasionally making notes in one of the dozens of steno pads she kept in her desk, and coaxing the most amazing things from the ether. When she wasn't doing that, she was on the phone with one of her dozens of contacts around the area, secretaries and personal assistants to just about anyone who mattered, coaxing amazing things from them as well. If she was bored we were in trouble.

"We heard anything from Holcombe, Stein and Chang?" I asked.

"Not a peep. I think they're all too busy planning their summer vacations."

Quincy and his partners often took most of July off. They'd take their staff, the legal clerks, associates, and secretaries, off to some resort somewhere for a few weeks' retreat. Most often, their destination would be Las Vegas or Reno, both cities hotter any time of year than

Washington, DC at its hottest, but with casinos, swimming pools, and extravagant shows to take their minds off the heat. I don't remember the last time I took a vacation longer than a weekend. I don't remember Heather taking even that.

"Maybe we should take vacations," I said.

She cocked her head and looked at me, her right eye, a brilliant blue, almost hidden by a lock of her golden hair. "That's not a bad idea."

"Except, I don't know where I could afford to go, or where I'd even want to go for that matter."

I couldn't remember the last time I'd taken a proper vacation. Oh, Sandra and I had gone to the South Carolina beaches once or twice for the weekend, and we'd spent a few days in the mountains of West Virginia, but nothing that could really be called a *vacation*.

"You could ask Sandra," she said. "I'll bet now that school's out, she'd like to get away from the city for a week or two."

"I suppose I could do that. Where would you go?"

She cocked her head the other way, covering the other eye. I could see her thinking about it. "I have an aunt in St. Petersburg, Florida. I haven't seen her in a long time. I guess I could go visit her."

I'd been to St. Petersburg once, a long time back when I was in the army stationed at Fort Bragg. It wasn't bad, but it wasn't Miami Beach either.

"What would you do in St. Petersburg?"

"Well, my Aunt Sophie lives in one of those retirement communities. I guess I'd spend some time with her, you know, talking and catching up on the family. Maybe watch some TV. And, if I get really bored, go to the beach or something."

"Sounds exciting."

It didn't really.

"It beats sitting here watching you mope around with nothing to do but listen to the air conditioner."

I guess it did at that. "It's not my fault that the bad guys are staying inside and out of trouble because of the heat."

"Oh, I'll bet they're making trouble inside. We're just not hearing about it because people don't want to come outside to talk about it."

"Maybe the bad guys have gone south to Florida to make trouble on the beach."

She made a face at me. "I bought a new bikini last year and never got a chance to wear it."

"I'll bet you look good in a bikini."

"You think the bad guys would like it?"

Charles Ray

2.

With nothing to do at the office, I knocked off early and drove home. The heat rose in waves all around me as I drove, causing the scene scrolling past my windows to look shimmery, and my Mustang's air conditioner complained at being run at maximum to chase the heat out of the car. It was overdue for service, but I didn't feel like standing around a hot garage while some sweaty mechanic found three or four things wrong that would take several hundred dollars out of my bank account to fix. We weren't tapped out yet, but if we didn't get a client soon, it wouldn't be healthy. Besides, if I didn't take it in, they couldn't find anything wrong. It's sort of like not going to the doctor. If they don't tell you something's wrong with you, you're healthy, right?

District schools had closed for the summer

the previous week, leaving Sandra with little to do but hang around the house. She was lounging on the sofa when I came in, wearing a pair of blue, crotch hugging shorts and a T-shirt. She didn't have a bra on, and her breasts were straining against the flimsy material.

Sandra looks good in anything, with an athletic, well-toned body and flawless skin, the less, in fact, the better. She's normally looking at the world through round, wide-set, azure eyes that twinkle in the light, but stretched out on the couch, fanning herself with a copy of *Newsweek*, she just looked bored.

"You're home," she said.

I felt a slight tingle at the nape of my neck. Sandra's not given to making stupidly obvious statements. Something was bothering her.

"Yeah, what's up, babe?"

I learned a long time ago, with my wife Sarah in fact, that it's sometimes best to approach these situations delicately and indirectly. If I opened the door wide enough, she'd tell me what was bugging her, but only if I opened it slowly.

"Never thought I'd miss a bunch of noisy teenagers," she said.

"I take that to mean you couldn't find anything interesting to do all day."

She fanned harder. "It was too hot to go outside, so I couldn't even take my frustrations out on the heavy bag in the barn. By the way, the air conditioning's not really putting out as much cool air as it should."

I could see that. The fine sheen of perspiration on her body had caused the T-shirt to become almost transparent in some strategic locations. The view wasn't bad.

"Would you like a cup of hot tea?"

She stopped fanning. Both of her blue orbs pierced through me. "Are you kidding? I'm not too hot yet, but I don't see how drinking hot tea will help."

"Hey, babe, remember once I told you, when your body's hot on the outside, drinking warm liquids causes it to try and compensate by cooling off on the inside. I learned that from an old sergeant when I was assigned to the Philippines."

She gave me a skeptical look.

"No kidding, it really works. Look, just sit back and I'll go brew up a pot."

I left her sitting there and padded out to the kitchen. I normally prefer brewing my tea slowly, but I wasn't sure she had the patience to wait, so I zapped a cup of hot water in the microwave and sprinkled in some green tea leaves. By the time I got back to her on the sofa, the water had begun to darken. I blew on it, swirling the vapors, and handed it to her. "Sip it slowly," I said.

She put the cup to her lips and, looking up at me with those baby blues of hers, took a tentative sip. Then, she took another, and another. "Okay," she said after several sips. "I don't know if it'll make me feel cooler, but it does make me feel better. Thanks."

I leaned over and kissed her, first the top of her head, where her soft hair flowed off to the sides and I could see her scalp, and then her forehead, and finally, tilting her head back, on her luscious lips. As her lips parted, I could taste the residue of green tea on her tongue. "No thanks necessary," I said, as I pulled away. "I exist for your pleasure."

A look came into her eyes that I recognized, but, she frowned. "Afraid that will have to wait, hon," she said. "You know we have Quincy, Buster, Alma and the kids coming tonight. And, we should start getting things prepared, shouldn't we?"

Darn. I'd completely forgotten that we'd promised to host a little back yard cookout. Buster and Alma would be bringing the twins, little Albert and Sandra, to let everyone see how they'd grown. They were approaching three now, talking, walking, and basically, I figured, a handful. Alma probably just wanted some free babysitting and a chance to talk to adults for a change. Buster had been doing a lot of overtime, leaving her alone with the kids. His overtime was partly due to the always high DC crime rate, as much to his own desire to have grownups to deal with, even the lowlifes he met on the street.

As for me; I've never been all that good with kids. I was okay with my son, Ethan, but he died when he was just six, and most of his first six years I was off on one deployment or another to countries whose names you wouldn't recognize, or be able to find on a map.

Then, I remembered I hadn't invited Heather. Shit, she'd be devastated if she found out. "Babe, I forgot to include Heather. Could you call her and tell her to come. Tell her it was a last minute thing or something. Meanwhile, I'll set up the grill and stuff."

"Are we getting forgetful in our old age?" Sandra asked, laughing.

I didn't find it funny.

I went to the kitchen and drug the old grille out of the storage cabinet next to the refrigerator. I took it out to the back and set it up just off the porch. I then went to the barn and retrieved the picnic table that I hadn't used for a long time, dusted it off, and drug it over next to the porch. I went back to the barn and got a bag of charcoal I'd been keeping under the table and a bag of mesquite twigs I'd purchased at a local hardware chain store.

I put a double layer of the little lumps of charcoal in the grille and laid a layer of mesquite over that. I went back to the barn and picked up eight long poles, at the end of which were purplish globes. Bug zapper lamps. The kid at the hardware store said eight would be enough to keep bugs at bay in an area twice the size of my backyard. I hadn't tested them before. Has to be a first time for everything, I thought. It wasn't as if those who were coming weren't accustomed to the bugs that infest the night air in Washington during the warm season. If the damn bug zappers didn't work, we could always go inside.

3.

Buster and his family arrived at a quarter to seven, followed soon after by Heather who gave me a nasty frown as she walked in.

"So," she said. "It's a good thing Sandra remembered to call me. Did you forget you were having a barbecue tonight?"

What could I say? I had completely forgotten. I figured it was wise to just admit it. "Yeah, guess I did. Sorry, I guess the heat and having no cases to work on had my mind too preoccupied."

She made a snorting sound and walked over to Sandra, giving her a sisterly hug.

Over her shoulder, Sandra gave me a

sympathetic look.

The tense mood lightened, though, as soon as Heather's eyes fell on the twins. I hadn't seen them in several months, and they seemed to have doubled in size in that time. Except for Sandra's longer hair and a mischievous glint in her large brown eyes, they were like clones of each other, and they were absolutely devoted to each other. Where you saw one, the other was close at hand. As soon as Buster and Alma sat them down, they began exploring the living room, touching and tasting everything within reach. Little Sandra was clearly the alpha female of the duo, with Albert following her lead in everything, much like the relationship that existed between their parents. Buster beamed with pride as Sandra picked up an object and mumbled something unintelligible, probably giving it a name, and Albert would repeat what she said. Alma kept a wary eye on them, and whenever they approached anything that looked fragile or breakable, was at their sides in an instant, her brown fingers waving in their faces and a stern look on her otherwise cherubic face.

Quincy had called and informed us that he'd be a bit late, so I ushered everyone through the kitchen and onto the back porch.

The sun, though behind the trees, still lit up the evening sky. It wouldn't properly set until nearly nine. But, the bugs were getting an early start. The bug zappers were making z-z-zt!

Sounds as the large white moths wandered too close. This, of course, immediately attracted the twins' attention. They toddled to the edge of the porch, near one of the little poles, and gazed up at the violet globe, clapping their tiny brown hands at every z-z-zt!, and there were lots of them. Bugs are dumb – or, I thought, maybe they're just tired of the heat and are taking the easy way out.

I stepped off the porch and lit the charcoal which I'd previously soaked with starter fluid. I was rewarded with an immediate orange flame which just as quickly died down as the little black lumps glowed, red at first and then taking on a patina of gray. The mesquite twigs were ignited by the heat from the charcoal, glowing red and giving off the familiar sweet odor. I held my hand over the pile, feeling the heat radiating from it. It was at just the right temperature to cook the meat slowly.

I put the grille over the fire and ladled on several beef patties and frankfurters. The beef began to sizzle, and the frankfurters, despite my having scored them, curled up a bit. The smell of roasting meat mixed with the mesquite aroma tickled my nose. My mouth began to water.

Buster went back into the kitchen with Sandra, and the two of them soon returned cradling several chilled bottles of *dos equis* beer and two small plastic bottles of grape juice for the twins.

After opening two bottles, Buster sidled over to where I was tending the meat on the grille. "I hope you plannin' to do up a couple of thick steaks, bro," he said as he handed me one of the frosted bottles. "What you got there now just be a snack."

I took the bottle and tilting my head back, took a long swallow. It was my first of the day, and it felt good going down. "Sure, Buster," I said. "But, I thought I'd do hamburgers and hotdogs first, for the kids, you know."

He drank and smacked his lips. "Now, that do sound like a plan. Hey, what you plannin' to do for vacation this year?"

"I can't decide. I guess I'll probably let Sandra pick something. What about you guys?"

Buster laughed, low and growly, and bumped his half-empty beer bottle against my arm. "Damn if you ain't soundin' like a married man," he said. "Lettin' the little woman decide where to go on a trip." Then he looked around, fixing his gaze on Alma, who was wiping purple grape smears from little Albert's face. "Alma decided we'd maybe go over to Ocean City and rent a beach house for a week." He frowned.

"Sounds fun; why the long face?"

"I was kinda hopin' to go up to West Virginia and do some fishin' with Lum Kellum."

Kellum is sheriff in a little West Virginia town. Buster and I met him when a militia group that was based just outside his town kidnapped a pregnant Alma and Sandra. Why that dumb bunch of rednecks would do that is a long story that really doesn't matter. What matters is, they pissed me off, and I went after them. Buster went with me, and Kellum threw in with us. We'd become friends after that, and, being fellow officers of the law, he and Buster had really hit it off.

"Maybe you could compromise," I said. "Spend two or three days at the beach, and then go up to the mountains for fishing for two or three days."

"Dang; never thought of that. You one smart dude, you know that."

Well, of course I knew that. It's always easy to solve someone else's problems.

Everyone's attention was drawn to a tall figure coming around the corner of the house. Quincy had finally arrived. He was carrying two six packs of *Corona*, my other favorite Mexican beer, one in each hand.

"Hey, I heard the commotion," he said. "Looks like you took me seriously about starting without me."

Sandra walked over, pecked him on the cheek and relieved him of the beer, which she put in the cooler. "We haven't started eating yet, Quince. Would you like something to drink while we wait for Al to burn the food?"

Quincy took a *dos equis* from the cooler, took off the cap, and took a long drink. He thanked Sandra and then walked over to where Buster and I were standing over the grille.

Dressed in khaki pants and a light green shirt, opened at the collar, he looked like anything but the highly-paid lawyer that he was. He's my height, but about twenty pounds lighter and not quite as broad in the chest. Narrow at the waist, he also doesn't have my problem of having to watch out for middle age spread, even though he's only a year younger. His straight black hair, combed back over his head, doesn't have a hint of gray. Dark, almond-shaped eyes under thin dark brows look at the world with a hint of skepticism, but his thin lips are always curved slightly upward in a shy smile.

"Hey, guys, what's up?" he asked.

He looked at Buster as he spoke. I noticed that he avoided eye contact with me. That was a sure sign that he had something on his mind that pertained to me, and was working up the nerve to bring it up. Perhaps, I thought, a last minute case for his firm. One that I probably wouldn't like, like the time he sent me to southern Virginia to contact a runaway bride and deliver a letter from her husband. I've found it best to let him work it out.

"Nothing much," I said. "You want hamburger or hotdog? Or, would you rather wait until I do the steaks?"

"Maybe I'll prime the pump with a hotdog, and then grab one of the steaks," he said.

He definitely had something on his mind. Quincy, unlike Buster, is not a voracious eater. Like Heather, he tends to salads and other healthy stuff, which is why his waist stays so trim.

"What's up with you legal types?" Buster asked.

"Not much. In fact, we're planning to shut the firm down for a month and take our staff on a retreat."

"Going to Vegas again?" I asked.

"Yeah, they are. But, this year, I'll be going elsewhere."

"Not going to Sin City with the rest?" I asked, feigning surprise. "Where would you be going that's more fun than Vegas?"

"It's not exactly more fun. I never told you about my relatives who live in Hawaii, did I?"

He'd never told me much about any of his relatives. I knew that his parents lived on the

West Coast, but we never spoke of them much.

"No, you didn't."

"Well, see, I have this uncle in Hawaii. Gordon Liu. He owns several plantations on the big island, mostly growing pineapples for the big canneries. His eldest daughter, my cousin Amy, is getting married, and I've been invited to the wedding."

"Aw, man," Buster said. "That don't sound like fun to me."

Quincy shrugged. "No, but family obligations can't be ignored. I'd never hear the last of it if I refused to go."

Except for a few distant cousins back in Texas where I grew up, I had no family obligations to deal with, but I knew the importance of family to Asians, even those, like Quincy's family, who've lived in the U.S. for generations.

"Well, it's just a wedding," I said. "That can't be more than a few days out of your summer."

"I wish," he said. "They're doing it at some secluded resort on Maui instead of their home on Hawaii. Uncle Gordon called me yesterday and said they're planning a week-long celebration. Amy's their eldest and she turns thirty soon, so getting her married off is a big deal."

The women had wandered into our vicinity, along with the twins who had been drawn away from the spectacle of self-immolating bugs by the smell of the meat that was just about ready. I tossed some hamburger buns and hot dog rolls on the grille to toast.

"So," I said. "It doesn't sound all that bad to me. You get to spend time at a ritzy Hawaiian resort. Why not just plan to enjoy it?"

Quincy's lips turned down. His brow furrowed. "You don't understand, Al. My parents will be there, too. There's no way I'll be enjoying myself. I'm nearing fifty and still not married. My mom and Aunt Penny will bug the hell out of me every minute. Oh, it'll be subtle, but, they'll be constantly reminding me that I've not fulfilled my filial obligation to ensure continuation of the family line."

"Oh, you poor thing," Sandra said. "I wish there was something we could do to help you."

That's Sandra, always wanting to pick up strays, to solve all the world's problems. There are some problems, and family problems of other people head my list, that you don't really want to get in the middle of.

"Well," said Quincy. "There is a way you could help."

I didn't like where this conversation was going.

"What can we do to help?" Sandra asked.

Nothing, absolutely nothing, my mind screamed. But, I kept my mouth clamped tight.

There was a twinkle in Quincy's eyes. I didn't like that look.

"There is one thing," he said. "If there was something, or someone, else there to distract their attention, maybe my mom and aunt wouldn't have a chance to bug me so much."

"Something? Someone?" Sandra asked, all innocent like. "Like what; or who?"

Oh, I really didn't like where this was going. I didn't like it at all.

"Well," he said. "I was thinking, if you and Al came along; him being a famous private detective and all, maybe they'd be so fascinated by his stories they'd ignore me."

"Uh, I'm not so sure about that," I said. "The last time we went on a vacation with you, we ended up spending the weekend stranded on an island with a corpse."

That had been the time Sandra and I'd gone with Quincy and some of his wealthy friends on a retreat on Chesapeake Bay that had turned deadly when a love triangle went awry.

"Oh, I promise you there'll be nothing like that this time. This will just be my family and a few close family friends."

"Yeah, but Hawaii is nothing but a bunch of islands, and islands mean boats," I said. "You know how I hate boats."

"Oh, there'll be no boats this time, cross my heart. We'll be flying from Honolulu to Maui, and the resort is well inland away from the beach."

I sensed from the way Sandra's face was lighting up that I was losing this fight. But, I decided to go down swinging. "I don't know, buddy. Going all the way to Hawaii at this time of year; that has to be expensive. I'm not sure we can afford it."

"No problem there," he said. "I asked my uncle if I could bring some friends, and he's agreed to buy our tickets. He's also paying all the expenses at the spa."

"Spa?" Sandra asked. "As in vacation spa, with saunas and massages and stuff like that?"

"Yeah, and it's really private, too, according to Uncle Gordon. Got a private helipad, swimming pool, and great views of the mountains of Maui. Everyone will have their own private cabana, and the food's the best in the islands."

Do you know the feeling of going down in flames, your aircraft disintegrating all around you and your ejection seat is malfunctioning?

Being in the middle of the ocean, your boat's leaking, and you never learned to swim; and, by the way, you're being circled by dozens of hungry sharks? Me neither, but at that moment I had an inkling of how that must feel. Sandra's eyes had lit up. A broad smile illuminated her face.

I was going to Hawaii to be a guest at a wedding of people I'd never met. Despite what Quincy said, I had this vision of being on a boat at some point, and I hate boats.

I would have to make small talk with these strangers, and, since many of them would be Quincy's relatives, and he *was* one of my few best friends, I'd have to mind my manners and make nice with them.

The only bright spot was that I knew Sandra looked good in a bikini. Well, there was one other nice thing – someone else would be paying for it.

4.

The thing about having a determined, desperate friend and a decisive girl friend is, once they've set their mind on you doing something, you find yourself in the middle of it before you've had a chance to even clearly understand what it is you've gotten yourself in the middle of.

That, anyway, is how I felt two days later, as I belted myself into seat 20D of the United Airlines Boeing 737 just before it pulled away from the gate at Dulles Airport. Quincy, a smug look on his face, sat across the aisle from me in 20C, and Sandra sat next to me in 20E, her head resting on my shoulder.

The plane, bound for San Francisco, where we'd have to change planes for our final jump to Honolulu, was full, and we'd been lucky to get exit row seats, which enabled Quincy and I to stretch out our legs. Sandra's a tall woman, too, and would have suffered as much as the two of us had we been crammed into regular seats. Most of the other passengers were college students going home for summer, families getting an early start on summer vacation, and a few buttoned-down business types. Most of the latter were in front of us in the little business class section of the plane, where they got drinks served while we waited to take off, and had seats that were a bit wider.

If there's anything I dislike more than being on a boat, it's being on an airplane. Something about being enclosed in a tin can, miles above the earth, hurtling through the air with just a few inches of fragile metal between you and - , I tried not to think about it as the air system hummed, bathing us with recycled air that smelled faintly of industrial detergent.

Sandra kept her head against my shoulder throughout the five-hour flight except when they served a light meal somewhere over Kansas. I picked at my food, but we'd eaten a late breakfast before Heather had come by and taken us to the airport, so most of it was left uneaten on the tray. The flight attendant, a shapely redhead with a generous scattering of freckles on her pale face, gave me a concerned look when she took the trays away at the end of the meal service.

Quincy had eaten all of his meal, and as soon as the empty tray was taken away, had put his seat back a bit and dropped off to sleep. Sandra put her head back against my shoulder and was quickly making little bubbling noises. Despite having eaten only a little, I couldn't sleep, so I just sat there looking up at the off-color display on the little television screen suspended from the ceiling. I didn't bother with the earphones. The movie that was playing didn't look all that interesting.

Over the Sierras, we skirted around the edge of an electrical storm. It would probably have looked fantastic at night, if you're into pyrotechnic displays. It only worried me. Jagged spears of lightning, stabbing from the billowing black clouds off in the distance didn't make me feel comfortable. We were zipping along in a metal container, and metal attracts lightning. I know commercial aircraft have systems to protect against lightning strikes, but when you're strapped in a seat, with nowhere to go, your mind tends to ignore rational things like that.

When we started our descent into San Francisco's airport, I felt my ears pop from the change in air pressure, and a dipping sensation. Beside me, Sandra stirred.

"Are we there yet?" she asked sleepily.

"No, we're just landing in San Francisco. We

have to change planes here for five more hours of flying to Honolulu."

"Oh," she said, and put her head back on my shoulder, instantly asleep.

I don't know how she does it.

The landing was smooth and uneventful. We made our way from the arrival gate, across the terminal to our departure gate, and found we had to wait for an hour. Sandra and I decided to just hang out there, but, Quincy wandered off in search of a newsstand, returning a few minutes later with copies of the *Wall Street Journal*, *Newsweek*, and the *New York Times* tucked under his arm.

"You worried they won't have newspapers in Hawaii?" I asked.

"We're only going to be in Honolulu for a short while; no time to pick up on reading material," he said. "Where we'll be on Maui there aren't any newsstands. And, no cable TV either."

"I thought the idea of a vacation was to get away from work."

"Yeah, but I don't want to be completely cut off from the world."

He then proceeded to read through each of the publications, negating any value they'd have once we reached our destination. The *Journal* and the *Times* went into the big brown recycle bin as we prepared to board. I guess there was an article in *Newsweek* he wanted to re-read.

Like our flight from Washington, the San Francisco-Honolulu flight was full. A large group of college students, many of them wearing polo shirts with surfer slogans, and a group of ten young military recruits with stiffly pressed uniforms and close-cropped hair on their way to assignment in Okinawa by way of Hawaii.

I remembered the days when I, as a young officer, had transited Hawaii on my way to one or another of our outposts scattered across the Pacific and Asia. A rest stop in Honolulu, with a tiny room at the BOQ located on Hickham Air Force Base, adjacent to the airport, and a trip to downtown Honolulu to Hotel Street and its blocks of nudie bars filled with GIs and Japanese businessmen vying with each other for the attention of the topless and bottomless dancers with their undulating pelvises and vacant stares, only looking animated when someone stuffed tens or twenties into their G strings, or in other convenient slots. This had been back in the 70s and early 80s, and I'd read somewhere that Hotel Street had been cleaned up as the islands tried to rebrand themselves as a great family tourist destination. There were still nudie bars, but they were no longer blatantly advertised, and were often in dingy side streets, and even there, the acts were no longer as explicit as in the old days. Everything changes.

One thing that hadn't changed too much was the fact that five hours flying from San Francisco to Hawaii, once the mainland coast had faded into the background, can be the most boring five hours of your life. The three of us had been seated together, and Quincy and I had agreed to rotate between the window seat and the aisle to give each other leg stretching room. In addition to the lack of knee space, the window seat gives you a view of the outside, and from 35,000 feet, the ocean that can be glimpsed through the cloud layer, or the cloud layer itself, takes on a boring sameness than would have lulled me to sleep, if I'd been able to sleep on a plane in flight, which I'm not.

The movie was yet another boring film that I had no desire to subject myself to, so I decided to see if the music selection would help me pass the time. The jazz channel had some nice selections, which kept me amused for the first ninety minutes, but when it started back at the first selection, as much as I like Coltrane and Gillespie, I was bored again. And the little plugs on the airline earphones are really annoying after a few minutes.

I tried reading the inflight magazine, but none of the articles interested me. It took me fifteen minutes to complete all the puzzles. In a word, I was wishing I was back in my office. I'd still be bored, but I'd be on the ground.

One thing about the flights to Hawaii that does provide a bit diversion is the little contest they run. They announce flight speed, and some other navigation data, and then challenge passengers to estimate when the plane will reach the midway point in the flight. I worked it out to within five minutes, but a lady several rows behind me had figured it out to the precise minute. She got a certificate for some gift at one of the shops on Waikiki, and I was left with two and a half hours of empty time to fill.

It was nearly seven pm, and the sun was a tangerine-colored oval low in the western sky when we swung around Diamond Head for our final approach to Honolulu International Airport. We flew over Oahu, with Waikiki Beach and the downtown area off our left wing, over Pearl Harbor, with the stark white of the U.S.S. Arizona Memorial clear against the still blue water sliding below the right wing, and then the plane dipped left, swung around, and glided to a landing.

We made our way to the sidewalk in front of the terminal and boarded one of the shuttle buses that ran along in front of the terminals to the baggage claim area near the front of the airport.

A medium height, suntanned man wearing a gaudy shirt and holding three of the flower *leis* with which Hawaiians welcome visitors, came toward us as we stepped down from the shuttle.

"Aloha, brah," he said, as he neared. "You must be Quincy Chang, and these be your friends. I'm Kono Waihulu, general manager of Xanadu. Your uncle sent me to fetch you."

All this was said in a rapid fire manner as he slipped the *leis* over our heads, giving Sandra a peck on the cheek as he gave her hers.

"Huh?" Was all Quincy could say.

"You give me your luggage claim check, and I see to the bags," he said, holding out his hand. "We go straight to interisland terminal for flight to Maui."

We handed over our claim tickets, which he turned and gave to a slump-shouldered man who had been hovering near. The old man scurried off in the direction of the baggage carousels.

"Why couldn't we have just checked out bags through to Maui?" I asked.

"Ah, bruddah, we not goin' by dem regular schedule flight. Mr. Liu he done chartered whirlybird for take us."

Okay, I don't like boats, and I'm not fond of flying in airplanes, but I really, really don't like flying in helicopters, especially when it's dark, and it was already after seven, with the sun a mere arc as it sank behind the mountains to the west.

"How long from here to Maui?" I asked. "Won't we be flying in the dark? Is that safe?"

Waihulu, or Kono, as he insisted we call him, gave me a sympathetic look. "You don't like flying, eh? A moke like you, 'fraid of airplanes?"

I wasn't sure he hadn't insulted me, but he was right; damn right I'm afraid of a craft that's not even supposed to be able to stay in the air, flying through the dark, over water, and with the potential of slamming into the side of a mountain. I didn't say any of this, though; just stared at him.

"Don't worry," he said. "We'll be on the ground in Maui before it's too dark, and the pilot's done this run hundreds of time without incident."

I noticed that his pidgin had disappeared.

"Okay, I'll take your word for it," I said.

"If it makes you feel any better, I'll be on the chopper with you."

It didn't make me feel any better, but Sandra and Quincy had already started following him into the terminal.

Our bags beat us there; probably some

interior passageway available to those with the proper identification; and were loaded on the helicopter that sat just outside the terminal building on the parking ramp. It was large, painted brilliant red, white and blue, with a huge pineapple painted on the fuselage, and the name 'Pineapple Express' on the tail. Inside it was nice; four seats on each side behind the cockpit, covered in soft leather and as wide as the easy chair in my living room back home. Kono got into the empty seat next to the pilot, another Hawaiian wearing dark aviator glasses and a brown vest over his Hawaiian shirt. I hoped he planned to remove the glasses when we took off.

5.

As soon as we were buckled in, the helicopter lifted off the tarmac, and after taxiing alongside the runway, angled up to cruise altitude, flying over Pearl Harbor low enough to make out figures in the last tour boats leaving the monument near the middle of the harbor. The monument itself, a brilliant white marble replication of a battleship's bridge, was bathed in the glow of several giant spotlights.

As we gained altitude, we flew out over the harbor, with Nimitz Highway below us to the left, over the industrial district leading into Honolulu from the airport. The squat gray buildings quickly gave way to shopping malls and high rises lining the streets, with the lights of cars darting into and out of the area leading to Waikiki Beach. The beach at this time of day was a light brown strip, dotted with circles of beach umbrellas that hadn't been taken in, with a darker area to the left marking the hotels, bars, and restaurants that lined it, and the light blue of the Pacific Ocean with white fringes of the combers gently lapping the sand.

As Waikiki swept by beneath us, we flew low over Diamond Head, a hulking mesa with a large crater in the center of its top, and then out over Koko Head with its yacht anchorage. After that, the ocean, light blue at first, but darkening as we approached the center of the channel between Oahu and the elongated island of Molokai, loomed beneath us. A few dark, knife-like shapes of boats, with light trails behind them, could be seen cutting through the water.

It didn't take long to traverse the 26-mile channel. Molokai, a long, dragon shape, its dark mountains jutting up like spikes on a dragon's back, touched the fluffy clouds that hung over the island. Here and there along the coast, I could see the lights of the small communities nestled there, but the rest of the island, as the light from the setting sun faded, was dark and forbidding looking as we passed to the south.

The channel between Molokai and Maui, our destination, was around 20 miles or so, and very quickly through the scratched Perspex windows I could see the two mountains at the west side of the blob-shaped island, thrusting up toward the darkening sky. Like Molokai, there were scattered groupings of lights along the coastline, marking the few settlements, and as we neared the island from the southwest, I could see dim lights scattered about the flat plain nestled between the western mountains and the peak to the east.

We swung past the two western mountains and the helicopter banked gently left and swung up over the plain, and then left again, aiming at the narrow valley between the two looming peaks. It was fully dark now, and the only thing I could see was the two mountains to either side, dark, ominous shapes against the darkening sky.

I'm not a white-knuckle flyer, but during my time in the army I saw more than one helicopter dashed against the side of a mountain while flying at night. I had no idea if the pilot of our craft knew what he was doing. In the green glow from his heads-up display, I could see that he was craning his neck to see ahead. At least he'd taken off his sunglasses.

Kono, his face looking ghostlike in the green light, turned and smiled at me.

"No worries, man," he shouted to make himself heard over the hum of the engines. "We be there soon. Harry here's done this flight a hundred times."

I smiled back at him and nodded. Wasn't

anything I could do about it now, so I figured I might as well relax and try to enjoy the rest of the flight. Sitting across from me, Sandra had her head against the headrest of the seat, her eyes closed. Quincy, sitting behind her, had the reading light pulled out and was scanning the magazine he'd hung on to.

I sat back and glanced out the window. Damn, those mountains looked awful close in the dark. What I wouldn't have given for a pair of night vision goggles so I could tell just how close.

After what seemed like an eternity, I could feel the helicopter losing altitude. In the distance ahead I could see three bright lights set in a triangle. Off to the left were more lights scattered around against the dark backdrop of the mountains.

We swooped in over a stand of towering trees and the pilot brought the craft to a hover and slowly lowered it. I felt a slight bump as we made contact with terra firma, and breathed a sigh of relief.

Before the rotors stopped spinning, Kono had unbuckled and hopped out. Suddenly, the place was alive with men and women wearing shorts and Hawaiian shirts, hauling our luggage off and placing them in two golf carts that were parked off to the side.

As I helped Sandra to the concrete pad upon

which we'd landed, Kono walked up beside me. "You okay, man?"

"Sure, no problem," I said. I looked at my watch. It was a quarter to nine.

"I don't know if you folks got fed on the plane, but if you're hungry, we can grab a quick bite up at the reception building before I show you to your cabanas."

"I could use something," Sandra said.

"Me too," Quincy quickly chimed in.

I hadn't eaten much on the flight from San Francisco, and now that I was safely on the ground I realized that I was hungry too.

Kono piled us into a golf cart modified to hold four passengers, and, jumping behind the wheel, drove us at breakneck speed toward a large building about a hundred yards upslope from the helipad. Behind me I could hear the whine of the engines as the helicopter began lifting off.

"The pilot's not staying the night here?" I asked.

"No, he lives in Kahului, east of here on the north side of the island. He wants to get home to his wife and kids."

"Is that the only way to get up here?"

"No, man," he said. "There's a road down the

mountain, goes all the way to Kahului. It's full of potholes, though, and nobody in his right mind uses it at night. Welcome to Xanadu."

6.

The reception building, a large one-story structure with a palm thatch roof held up by large dark wooden columns, was well lit. Teak tables were arranged around a large open space open to the night air, and there was a sweet smell that tickled at my nose. Torches set at an angle from some of the columns flickered and cast wavering shadows, but there were also fluorescent fixtures suspended from the rafters beneath the palm thatch. From somewhere I could hear the hum of a generator.

A couple of slim-waisted girls wearing body hugging flower print one piece dressed that stopped at mid-thigh, their flowing jet black hair festooned with bright red blossoms, and their golden thighs reflecting the light from the torches, offered us large glasses of some golden liquid. It tasted like pineapple and mango with a tang of some alcohol that I couldn't identify. They showed us to tables at the edge of the room and with a provocative swaying of slim hips, withdrew to fetch our food. Even Sandra watched them appreciatively as they walked away.

"This might not be such a bad vacation after all," Quincy said with a wistful look on his face.

We were sipping at our drinks when Kono joined us.

"So, folks, what do you think of Xanadu?"

"It's appropriately named," Sandra said. "But, where are the other guests?"

"Oh, we're usually full up this time of year, but Mr. Liu booked the place for the week for his daughter's wedding. There'll be about fifty guests; some of them arrived this morning, and the rest come tomorrow morning. We're only at about sixty percent capacity, but he's paying enough to make up the difference."

I looked at Quincy who kept his eyes on his drink.

"So," I said. "This uncle of yours is not just rich; he's filthy rich, eh?"

"Mr. Liu is one of the richest men on Maui, in all of Hawaii actually," Kono said. "He owns half the sugar plantations on the island, I think, and two big sugar mills down in Kahului."

Quincy's cheeks darkened. "Yeah, he's got money," he said. "And, while I like him and Aunt Penny well enough, it's a drag the way he's always flaunting his wealth."

"If you've got it, might as well flaunt it," Sandra said.

Just then, the two Hawaiian dolls came back, bearing trays, one with a tray of assorted fruits, pineapple, mango, guava, kiwi fruit, and some berries that I didn't recognize, the other with a tray laden with spring rolls, little meat balls, and tiny sausages wrapped in some kind of golden brown crusty covering. They put the trays into the center of the table and stepped back, their golden arms folded beneath their perky breasts which were barely contained within the floral print wraparounds they wore wrapped around their deliciously curved golden bodies.

"Just some *pupu* to cut the hunger before bed," Kono said.

Sandra, her fingers about to curl around a spring roll, stopped her hand in midair and stared at him, wide-eyed. "Some what?" she asked.

He laughed. "*Pupu*; that's Hawaiian for snacks. Oh, I see what you mean. Never thought about that. You *haole* really have some strange verbal concepts."

By now, his pidgin had totally vanished. I guess we were no longer categorized as tourists who he had to stay in character for.

Kono sat back, with his arms across his chest, and watched us devour, destroy, devastate the trays of *pupu*. I couldn't help but smile as Sandra, tentatively at first, finally ignored the unfortunateness of the name, sampled a bit of this and a piece of that, until finally, she was gorging herself.

After the trays were empty except for a few toothpicks, we sat back and had another of the fruity concoctions. By the time Kono escorted us to our cabanas, the alcohol in the drink had stoked a warm fire in my gut; a pleasant feeling.

The cabana was made from the same material as the reception building, just on a smaller scale. Polished wood floors, palm frond roofs, and, thankfully, walls instead of the open plan. The door even had a lock. Inside, it was divided into a sitting room, a spacious bedroom with a large bath, and a little nook with a small fridge and a microwave. No radio and no TV, but I don't imagine that people who stay at places like Xanadu plan to watch much TV.

I let Sandra shower first, and as she toweled off and put on a pair of shorts and a semi-transparent tee, I showered. I dried off and slipped on a pair of boxers and slid between the silk sheets. Sandra was already in bed, on her back, staring up at the ceiling fan that was making lazy circles above the bed.

I kissed her lightly on the lips, flipped off the light and lay back. The gentle lapping sound of the bit wooden fan blades was soothing, as was the music of the night birds in the nearby rain forest. Even the steady hum of the generator seemed designed to rock me to sleep.

Then, the bed shook as Sandra contorted her body, first one way, then another. After the shaking of the bed subsided, I felt the warmth of her bare thigh sliding across mine, and her soft hand as it eased across my stomach and then down toward the elastic waistband of my shorts. I felt the warmth of her breath against my neck just before her soft lips gently brushed my ear lobe.

"I'm not sleepy," she whispered huskily into my ear.

Charles Ray

7.

I woke up early the next morning, slipped out of bed, put on a pair of shorts and a tee and my old running shoes, and went outside.

In the morning light, I could see that Xanadu was set on a wide ridge that jutted out from the northern peak, about halfway up. It was surrounded on two sides by forest, one by the sharply rising mountain, and a fourth side that was lightly forested with glimpses of the narrow valley and the southern mountain beyond. There appeared to be about thirty of the cabanas spread in a semi-circle around the central reception building that was also a restaurant and lounge. A large rectangular swimming pool was on the west side of the central building. The cabanas, each with its own little tropical garden and patio, were connected by a gravel path just wide enough for a golf cart to traverse, that wound serpentine-like, connecting up with the central structure. The trees, some more than a hundred feet high, with gnarled trunks festooned with dull orange lichen and a few light yellow and salmon colored blossoms at along the branches, cast gray and green shadows over the resort. Golden spears of morning sunlight slashed through openings in the trees. I could feel the moisture in the air, but it was a pleasant feeling.

Unfamiliar with the place, I decided to do a brisk walk rather than jog. I started at our cabana and walked the entire perimeter, ending up back at the cabana twenty minutes later. When I went inside, Sandra was just waking up. We decided on a little romp before showering and dressing for breakfast, so by the time we finally got down to the restaurant, Quincy was already there, along with two elderly Chinese couples, whom I took to be his parents and his uncle and aunt, two strikingly beautiful Chinese girls, one who looked to be about Sandra's age, and one in her late twenties, sitting at one table, and a broad-shouldered white guy with neatly trimmed brown hair, sitting with another brown haired man, a younger guy whose hair was in need of trimming, a blond man, broad shouldered like the first, and a slim woman with long brown hair that draped over her shoulders, sitting at an adjacent table.

As we approached, Quincy stood. "Dad,

mom, folks, these are my friends, Al Pennyback and Sandra Winter," he said. "Al, these are my parents." He indicated the slight Chinese man with wispy black hair combed back on a narrow skull and a tiny woman with her black hair tied back in a severe bun, who sat to either side of him. "My aunt and uncle, Gordon and Xiaoping Liu." Pointing at another older couple sitting across from him. "And, my cousins, Amy and Constance." The two women were obviously related, but Amy, the older had a more settled look about her. Constance, as she smiled up at me, had a mischievous gleam in her eyes.

"Pleased to meet you all," I said.

"Likewise," said Sandra.

Gordon Liu stood. His hair was black and full and he had the bearing of someone who was accustomed to command. "Welcome Mr. Pennyback, Ms. Winter. We are honored that you would grace us with your presence at this most auspicious occasion. I trust that you find your accommodations satisfactory."

"More than satisfactory," Sandra said.

"I'd like to introduce my future son-in-law and his friends," Liu said, waving toward the group at the other table. Four heads swiveled in our direction, and four heads bobbed. The young guy in need of a trim, unlike the others, didn't bother smiling. "This is Darren Culpepper." He pointed to the broad-shouldered guy. "His brother Marcus, and his friends, Mr. Lane Vandemeer and Miss Shelly Corwin."

We nodded in their direction.

"Father, shouldn't you invite Al and Sandra to have a seat so they can eat breakfast?" Amy Liu said.

"Oh yes, please forgive my lack of manners," he said. "Please join us."

I sat next to Quincy's mother, who smiled broadly up at me, and Sandra went over and sat next to Constance Liu. A waiter, a twin of one of the girls who'd served us the night before, came and brought coffee and tea and took our breakfast orders. There was a choice of Asian or Western breakfast. Quincy, Sandra, Constance Liu, and I ordered Western, the others ordered Asian. Sandra, Quincy, and I had coffee. Everyone else drank tea.

"How long have you and Al been a couple?" I heard Constance Liu ask.

"Constance, stop being so nosey," Amy said, slapping her younger sister's hand.

"Aw, come on, it's plain to see they're into each other. I'm just curious."

"It's none of your business." The older woman leaned forward and looked at Sandra. "Forgive my sister, Sandra. You wouldn't know she'd been raised in an Asian household, where good manners are the order of the day."

Sandra smiled back at her. "That's okay; it doesn't bother me. Al and I have been together for a couple of years now."

Constance Liu stuck her tongue out at her sister. "See, she doesn't mind. You're such a prude. I don't know how you and Darren ever met, much less decided to get married."

Amy's cheeks darkened.

"How did you two meet?" Constance asked Sandra.

"Well, that's a long story, and probably not appropriate for the breakfast table," Sandra said. "I'll tell you later."

Constance's eyes lit up and a broad smile illuminated her face. I focused my attention on the sausages and toast on my plate, and noticed that Quincy was doing the same. I could feel Mrs. Chang's dark eyes boring into the side of my face. When I looked around at her, she was studying me intently, her head cocked to one side. I felt like a biology class specimen under a microscope. Beyond her, I could see that Quincy was frowning and his cheeks were flush.

"You been a friend of my son long time," Mrs. Chang finally broke the silence.

"Uh, yes ma'am. Quincy and I met more

than ten years ago."

"You not married. Maybe you are reason he not marry?"

"Please, mother," Quincy said in a low, pleading voice.

"Only ask," she said. "Mr. Pennyback, why you not marry? If you good friend of my son, maybe that why he not marry."

That feeling of being a specimen grew stronger; only now, it felt more like an insect pinned to a board. "Well, ma'am, I was married once, but my wife died."

Her face wrinkled up and she got a sad look in her eyes. She patted my hand. She then turned to Quincy. "So, you not follow example of your friend. He marry and stay with wife until she die. Why you no marry yet?"

The 'whup-whup' sounds of a helicopter coming in for a landing spared Quincy. Everyone got up and went to the side of the restaurant from which there was a clear view of the helipad. In the morning light, the EC225, painted in red, white, and blue, complete with the pineapple on the fuselage, looked like the one that had brought us, but, then I could see a second, identical craft circling above, waiting for this one to disgorge its passengers and clear the pad. Obviously the Pineapple Express was more than a single aircraft operation.

Twelve people, Asian and White, mostly couples, got off the aircraft. The ground crew, young Hawaiians in khaki shorts and flowery shirts, made quick work of transferring their baggage to four waiting golf carts. The second craft was on the ground as soon as the first had cleared it, and the operation repeated itself.

"That would be most of the rest of our guests," Gordon Liu said. He was standing near me. "The tall gray-haired man is the preacher who will be doing the ceremony, Father Lawrence Dao, he is in charge of the parish near our factory." He pointed to a tall, distinguished looking Asian man, with iron-gray hair that swept in wings at the sides of his head, and whose clerical collar was clearly visible under his dark jacket.

My gaze, though, was drawn past him to the figure that followed him. She was tall, half a head taller than the priest, wearing flowered shorts that clung to long, shapely, bronzed legs, and a bright blue shirt, opened and exposing the round cleavage of large breasts. The way the shirt flashed and swayed as she walked it was clear that those breasts were unencumbered by a bra. On shapely feet she wore rope sandals. Her hips swayed languidly as she kept pace with the priest. She had red hair piled high on her head, with a bright red poinsettia set just above her right ear.

I sensed Gordon Liu at my side, watching

me watch the girl. Conscious that I was his guest, and I just might be ogling some female member of his family, I tore my gaze away and looked at him.

"So, this will be a Catholic service?" Not that it mattered, but I felt the need to make some kind of conversation.

"Yes, Darren is Catholic," he said. "We're Buddhist, but Amy met him when they were students at Stanford, and when they became engaged, she converted." His matter of fact tone told me he, like me, just felt the need to make conversation. That it really didn't matter.

We returned to the table. We'd nearly finished eating when the arrival of the helicopters interrupted us, and the party was beginning to break up. Sandra and the Liu sisters were deep in conversation, and Quincy was huddled with his mother. I stood and started toward the exit.

Darren Culpepper stood and blocked me. He stuck out his hand. Broad faced, with open, guileless blue eyes and a shy smile, I instantly liked him.

"We weren't really properly introduced," he said. "Darren Culpepper."

"Al Pennyback," I said. "I'm Quincy Chang's friend. He's your future bride's cousin."

"Yeah, I know him. You were in the army,

right?"

"Uh, yes, I was. Quincy and I met in the army as a matter of fact. How did you know?"

"The way you carry yourself, alert to your surroundings, sort of erect, but relaxed at the same time. I was in the military myself; the navy."

Now that he said it, I had noticed that he carried himself in a certain way suggesting prior exposure to military discipline. There was something in his eyes, a wariness that was all too familiar to me. "SEAL, right?"

"Is it that obvious?"

"I know the look."

"You were a Green Beret?"

I nodded. In that brief exchange, we'd established a bond. "I guess you can never get it out of your system. How long you been out?"

"Six months," he said. "When my dad died, I decided it was time to do my duty to my family. I resigned my commission to take over the family business. My mom died when I was a teenager. There's just me and my brother, Marcus, now." He inclined his head toward the younger man who was sitting at their table staring morosely into his coffee. "Mark's got no head for business, so it's left to me to keep things together."

"So, the two of you are running the family business? What kind of business is it?"

I didn't really care, but it seemed the polite thing to do. Besides, other than Quincy and Sandra, he would be someone I could at least have a conversation with.

"We're in construction. We do a lot of the factories here in Hawaii, that and other industrial projects."

His face took on a pensive look.

"You miss the navy, don't you?"

"Damn right I do, but a higher duty calls. Lane there is a buddy from the navy. He's a former SEAL, too. I talked him into leaving the navy and joining me in running the business. The woman sitting next to him is Shelly Corwin. She's an environmental expert I met when I was stationed at San Diego. I'm bringing her on to help get the company on the right track."

"From SEAL to CEO; quite a transition for you. Must be a real challenge."

"You don't know the half of it," he said. "Hey, maybe we can get together later and shoot the shit over a few beers?"

I nodded, and we shook hands. He turned and walked away. For a man who was just about to get married, he looked very unhappy.

8.

The priest opened the door and stepped aside to allow the redhead to enter the restaurant. She glided through the door, her breasts still swaying. Up close, I could see that she was Asian, but with round Western eyes, eyes that were light gray that looked out on the world as if all they say belonged to her. Her lips were colored light pink and turned up at the sides in a slight smile as she advanced across the room toward Amy and Constance Liu.

"Mei Ling, you made it," Constance said, rushing over and pulling her into a tight embrace. "At last, I have somebody I can talk to."

"Nice seeing you too, babe," the redhead said, looking over the top of Constance's head at Quincy with a speculating glint in her eyes.

My eyes were mostly on her, but I paid enough attention to know that so was everyone else's, male and female. She was, I had to admit, the kind of woman who drew attention. Tall, shapely, self-possessed, and with an oval face and the kind of clear complexion that comes from a combination of good genes and lots of money spent on creams and oils.

Constance pulled away, holding the redhead's hand. "Folks, I'd like you to meet Mei Ling Chao," she said. "She and I work at the same model agency in LA."

So, she wasn't a relative. The frankly disapproving look on Mrs. Liu's face also said she wasn't very welcome. Gordon Liu, on the other hand, had a sappy smile on his face as he walked over, extending his hand. "Welcome, Miss Chao. Constance has spoken of you often."

Mei Ling Chao took his hand, but also bowed her head respectfully. "Liu xian sheng, it is an honor to finally meet you. Little Sister Constance has also spoken of you. I feel as if we have met before."

Liu beamed. The harsh look on his wife's face eased a fraction. I had to give her credit; Mei Ling Chao knew how to work people. But, as she spoke to Liu, her eyes never left Quincy who, by now, was aware of her scrutiny and looking uncomfortable.

Constance led her around, introducing her

in turn to each of us individually. Her gaze left Quincy for a few moments as she was introduced to me, but Sandra had by now moved to my side. The two women shared a glance, some unspoken communication passed between them. She smiled, nodded, gave my hand a final squeeze and moved on.

Constance saved Quincy for last. When she introduced him to Chao, the redhead held his hand much longer than she'd held mine, and stared into his eyes far longer; long enough to cause his cheeks to turn red. He kept looking past her at me with pleading in his eyes, like an animal that has been cornered by a larger, more ferocious beast. Poor Quincy; he was on the menu, and there was nothing I could do to help him. Mrs. Liu also saw what was happening, and her face was positively beaming now, as was Quincy's mother. Constance Liu stood there with an innocent look on her face. Boy, she was the best of them all. The manipulator, the one who'd set poor Quincy up; lined him up for slaughter as neatly as a cow being driven down a ramp toward the guy with the sledgehammer, and she had a Sunday School teacher expression on her face as if she was totally unaware of what was going on.

Charles Ray

9.

After an uncomfortable interval in the restaurant, the group broke up as the resort staff showed the newcomers to their rooms.

Sandra and I were on the way to our cabana when Quincy caught up with us near the swimming pool.

"Guys, hold up," he said. "You've got to help me."

Sandra put her face against my shoulder, shaking with barely suppressed giggling.

Quincy looked so forlorn, like he wanted to cry. "What's the problem, buddy?" I asked.

Sandra shook harder, and grabbed my bicep.

"They're ganging up on me. My mom, Amy, everybody! They put Constance up to inviting that friend of hers to the wedding. They're trying to get me to hook up with her."

His lips quivered, and his eyes glistened with held back tears. The big lug *was* on the verge of bawling.

"Come on, Quincy, Mei Ling is a beautiful woman," Sandra said. "You could do worse than having someone like that hanging on your arm for the week."

"It's what comes after the week that worries me," he said.

"How bad can it be?" I asked. "You treat her nice for the week, and then we go back to DC. A smart lawyer like you ought to be able to pull that off."

He looked at me, his expression one of incredulity. "Al, you don't understand how these women work. I say the wrong thing, do the wrong thing, and I'm hooked. Do you know how many ways there are to propose marriage in Chinese culture?" I shrugged. "Yeah, well neither do I. Hell, I could hold a chair for her and end up having that interpreted as a pledge of undying love. I tell you, I'm screwed, pal, unless you two can help me avoid her."

Sandra was laughing openly now. "Quincy, you're being a baby about this. Why not just relax and enjoy yourself?"

He regarded her with narrowed eyes. "You knew about this, didn't you?"

She feigned innocence. "Well, I might have heard Constance say something about it just before Mei Ling came in."

"You're on their side!"

"Aw, come on, Quincy," she said, holding her hands up in a defensive gesture. "I'm not on anyone's side. I just think you're overreacting."

He made a snorting sound, his gaze moving from her to me. "What about you, Al; you siding with them, too?"

"Hey, pal, you know you can count on me." I was treading on dangerous ground here, but friendship has to count for something. "I'll do what I can to run interference for you." I didn't think there was much I could do, but it was a lifeline, no matter how thin, to a man who was drowning.

"Thanks, Al," he said. He gave Sandra a stern look. "I knew I could depend on *you*. I guess for some people, the absence of a Y chromosome is more important than friendship."

He spun on his heels and walked toward his own cabana.

"He's really upset about this," I said to Sandra. "Why couldn't you show him a little more sympathy?"

"He could use a woman," she said. "They're just trying to do what's best for him."

"I think he should be the one to make that decision."

"Don't you think Mei Ling's pretty?"

"Hell, she's a knockout," I said. "But, even ice cream loses its taste when you're force fed."

"Meaning?"

"If Quince met her under different circumstances, he'd probably go for her. The mere fact that this was set up by his mother is a turn off. Babe, I don't know if you've noticed it, but except for his physical appearance, Quincy Chang is about as Chinese as I am."

She cocked her head to one side, a slender finger laid against her nose. "Oh my, that's true." She snapped her fingers. "Al, sweetheart, you go on to the room, I'll meet you later. I have something I have to do."

Before I could ask her what it was, she rushed off in the direction of the reception building. I had a twitchy feeling at the back of my neck.

The rest of the day went lazily by. The

Eurocopters kept shuttling more guests in, eight to twelve at a time, various Asian and white couples, from their early thirties to late-middle aged people, all looking prosperous as was befitting those who would receive invitations to such an exclusive event. Around mid-afternoon, a small, bubble-canopied chopper swung up the cut between the hills as if it was coming in for a landing, but, after making a couple of lazy circles around the resort, it flew on upwards, disappearing in the mist that hung over the mountains. Probably, I thought, a tourist, curious about the destination of the red, white, and blue aircraft that were landing there.

With little else to do, I decided to spend the rest of the day at the pool. Dressed in swimming trunks and with a *Spenser* novel to pass the time, I stretched out on one of the wicker lounges at pool's edge. Quincy, looking around as if he was being stalked, came out a few minutes later and pulled up a chair near me, where he lay back, leafing through his magazine.

The sky, a brilliant turquoise with scatterings of fluffy cumulus clouds except over the mountains, which were wreathed in a billowing gray mist, was relaxing.

I was just getting into Spenser's latest exploits when a shadow crept across the pages. I looked up. Darren Culpepper, wearing flowered swim trunks, his bronze chest covered with a light brown sprinkling of hair, stood there, looking down at me.

"Sorry if I'm bothering you," he said. "But, the women are fussing over the wedding dress, and I was beginning to feel like a fifth wheel. Mind if I join you?"

I dog-eared the page I'd been reading and put the book down on the tiled edge of the pool.

"No problem. Pull up a chair. I know how you feel. When I got married, I felt like an appendix myself." Sarah's father and the rest of her family had made a big fuss before our wedding, treating me like an interloper until the reverend said the words, "I now pronounce you man and wife." The most useless member of any wedding party is the groom, with nothing to do but say 'I do' at the appropriate time. "What's on your mind, other than pre-wedding jitters?"

He pulled an empty lounge next to me and draped his body over it, looking up at the sky.

"Oh, it's not that. I've resigned myself to being just a walk-on in this production. No, it's business that has my mind in turmoil right now."

"I should think that would be the least of your worries," I said. "After all, you're about to take over an already successful business, right?"

With furrowed brow, he proceeded to enlighten me. Yes, he said, the business was successful. His company, Culpepper Enterprises, had never been in the red, and looked to continue to prosper. His worry, though, was the environmental costs of that success. Many of the clients for whom they'd done construction projects were contributing to the degradation of the natural environment of Maui and the other islands where they operated, encroaching on natural habitats and contributing to the demise of plant and animal species for which the islands were famous. He felt an obligation to introduce changes to their business methods. While his father had been alive, such change had been impossible. The old man was from the old school. Only the bottom line counted. It was left to others to worry about the environment. His company was only responsible for delivering what the client wanted, on time and within budget – with a reasonable markup, of course.

When he'd resigned from the navy and agreed to take control of the company after his father died, he'd suggested changes to the board. Changes that had been resisted strongly; an element of the board, led by his brother, Marcus, were against his proposed changes, arguing that the environmental studies he was proposing were the responsibility of the clients, not the builder.

So far, he lamented, he'd only been able to make changes around the edges. He'd convinced his friend, Lane Vandemeer, to leave the navy and join him as Culpepper's chief operating officer, and then brought Shelly Corwin on as an advisor on environmental matters, moves that had earned him the enmity of opponents on his board.

"Sounds like you're fighting a holding action," I said when he'd finished.

"Yeah, but after the wedding, things will change. Amy's father gets it. He and I have discussed it, and he agrees that we need to take the long view. We can no longer let short-term profits blind us to the reality that if we destroy the environment, pretty soon there won't be any more profits. He's agreed to throw in with me and work to convince his colleagues in the sugar industry at least that adjustments need to be made."

"So, what's the problem? If you get the manufactures behind you, won't that cause your board to take a different view?"

"They won't have any choice. But, these guys are wedded to the old ways of doing things. They view any change as a threat that has to be resisted."

I shook my head. "That, my friend, is the very reason I've never wanted to be a part of the corporate world."

"Yeah, it makes some of the SEAL missions I've been on look like picnics, that's for sure." He laughed. But, there was no happiness in it.

Our conversation was interrupted by Mei Ling Chao's arrival. She'd changed her flowered shorts and blue shirt for a bikini. Two carmine strips that barely covered the essentials. Her red hair was pulled back and held in place by a blue ribbon, accenting her oval face, high forehead, and long neck. Her lips, tinted a darker red now, looked kissable, and her round eyes, accented with a touch of light purple, were like deep pools into which you wanted to dive. She glided rather than walked, her slender feet encased in black sandals made from what looked like rubber tires. We watched as she walked, her hips swaying, past us, past Quincy, who peeked at her over the top of his magazine, and around the pool to an empty lounge across from us, the curves of her buttocks undulating beneath the red strip. She lay back on the lounge, one leg up, the other stretched out, her hands at her sides. Closing her eyes, she lay there, letting the sun's rays caress her well-formed body, ignoring us.

I was torn between watching her – a pleasant activity, I must admit – and watching Quincy out of the corner of my eye. He continued to pretend that he was reading his magazine, but every few minutes, his gaze would stray in her direction, a puzzled look on his face.

Charles Ray

10.

The entire assembly gathered in the restaurant for dinner that night, over seventy people, for a pre-rehearsal dinner. There were toasts to the bride and groom, introductions all around – I didn't remember anyone's name – and tons of food and drink.

Around midnight it finally broke up, and people wandered off to their cabanas.

I woke up early the next morning and did four brisk circles around the perimeter of the resort, not really enough to work up a sweat, or even cause me to breathe hard, but better than inactivity. A couple of helicopters were coming up the valley. Shortly, one landed while the other circled. Hotel staff unloaded boxes and put them in the golf carts.

I finished my walk and walked to the pool. After a few minutes of meditation sitting on the tile edge of the pool, I went back to the cabana to shower.

Sandra woke up and joined me in the shower, and that made us late for breakfast. Constance Liu winked at Sandra as we entered the restaurant and did a little forefinger-thumb circle sign at her.

"What's that all about?" I asked.

"Nothing, dear," she said. "Let's get breakfast."

We selected food from a large breakfast buffet that had been arranged along one side of the room, and joined Quincy who was sitting alone at a table in the corner farthest from the entrance.

He had a plate of scrambled eggs, sausage, hash browns and toast in front of him, but, rather than eating, he was moving the food around on the plate as he glanced at Mei Ling Chao, sitting at a table near the center of the room with Amy and Constance.

"She is a beautiful woman, isn't she?" Sandra said as we sat our plates down.

Quincy started as if he'd been caught peeking through a hole in the wall of the girls' locker room. "Uh, who?" he said with a guilty look on his face.

"Why, Mei Ling, of course, and don't tell me you weren't looking at her."

"No, I wasn't . . . I was just trying to decide whether or not to order a second cup of coffee."

"But the one you have is still more than half full," Sandra said. "What's wrong with admitting you were looking at her?"

"Because I wasn't, that's all." He looked at me with a 'help me out here' expression on his face.

"Sorry, pal," I said. "It did look like you were checking her out. Hey, nothing wrong with that. Sandra's right; she's a looker."

"And," Sandra said. "You were wrong. She hasn't been trying to get her hooks into you. In fact, I'll bet your mother hasn't said a word to you about her, has she?"

"Uh, well, no actually, she hasn't."

I could imagine Sandra giving some her students the same look she was giving him. A look that said he'd been a victim of his own overactive imagination, and should listen to the teacher, because the teacher always knows best. "She's just a friend who happened to get an invitation to the wedding. No sneaky plans involving you at all."

Quincy's expression wavered, but there was still a hint of wariness in his eyes. He gave me a pleading look. "What do you think, Al? You think Sandra's right?"

"Certainly looks like it. I mean, she completely ignored you yesterday at the pool."

His glance went from me to her, and back to me.

"She is attractive," he said.

"That she is."

"I suppose it couldn't hurt to be nice to her."

"Not at all."

Sandra smiled.

Kono Waihulu walked into the restaurant. He had a worried look on his bronze face. He saw us in the corner and walked over. I could hear the throb of a helicopter taking off.

"Morning, Kono," Sandra said. "Why the long face?"

"Oh, a bit of troubling news," he said. "One of the tour choppers from Kahului went missing yesterday. Kid named Danny Kameahana was piloting it. Had some haole tourist with him. They didn't come back last night."

"Oh, my goodness; what do they think happened?"

"They don't know. There was no radio contact; but, up in these mountains you can get out of contact sometimes; and, he didn't file a detailed flight plan, so they're not even sure where to start looking. They're worried he might have had to land up in the mountains."

I didn't want to say what was going through my mind. If he was flying high enough, up where the mist was thick and visibility practically nil, there was a good chance a chance gust of wind could have driven the aircraft into the side of a hill. "Was it one of those little bubble front jobs?" I asked.

"Yeah, it was," Kono said.

"I saw one fly over yesterday. Headed up toward the top of the mountain to the north, but I lost sight of it in the clouds. That could have been your friend."

He brightened slightly. "You might be right. I'll call down to Kahului and tell them to check up that way. It's still a lot of territory to cover, and with the clouds they won't be able to see much from the air, but it's better than nothing."

He turned and left, wringing his hands. I knew what was going through his mind. During my army days, I'd sent men out on patrol, and then waited anxiously for them to return. Some never came back.

Charles Ray

11.

It was decided – well, actually, Mrs. Liu decided, as she was in charge of the actual ceremony – to have a rehearsal just before lunch.

Amy Liu had to argue with her mother for twenty minutes to convince her that it wouldn't be necessary for everyone to wear what they planned to wear for the real ceremony, which was planned for two days hence. She couldn't, however, get her to agree that all the guests didn't need to participate in the rehearsal. Mrs. Liu was leaving nothing to chance; she wanted to see how *everything* and *everyone* would look and act during the real thing, so, in assorted vacation garb, seventy people gathered on the well-manicured square of lawn adjacent to the swimming pool where ordinarily a couple of volleyball nets stood.

For the rehearsal, two banks of folding

chairs, each four across and stretching back ten deep, sat facing a small stage upon which had been affixed a wire frame archway, which I'd been told would be decorated with flowers and vines for the ceremony. For now, there were no flowers, no vines, just chairs and a four-by-six stage, six inches high.

I was wearing a pair of jeans and a polo shirt. Sandra wore a matching outfit, although I have to admit she looked better in it than I did. Mei Ling Chao showed up in a pink cheong sam with a slit up one side almost to her hip and a neckline that stopped just short of her navel. Quincy almost choked when he caught sight of her.

As she strolled languidly down the aisle between the chairs, exposing the golden flesh of her legs as the silk fabric slid aside, her breasts swaying, heads turned and eyes followed her movement. We were sitting four rows back from the front. She passed us, never looking down at us. I watched the rolling movement of her buttocks under the shiny fabric as she slid into the first chair two rows in front of us. Next to me, I heard Quincy's quick intake of breath.

Then, Darren Culpepper, dressed in dark brown pants and a white shirt, open at the throat, accompanied by his brother, wearing jeans and a gray sweater walked out from a small grove of azalea bushes behind the stage to take their place on the stage facing away from us. They were followed shortly by the priest, wearing a black suit with his gleaming white priest's collar, who stood in front of them.

The priest leaned forward and said something inaudible to Darren, and then he straightened and looked down at Mrs. Liu who was sitting on the front row two chairs in from the edge.

"This will be the start of the ceremony," he said to her. "Once we've taken our positions, the organist, will begin to play the wedding march, and the bride will be escorted in by her father."

"Why organist not here?" Mrs. Liu asked in a reedy voice. "We should practice music too."

A look of mild irritation creased the priest's face. "That won't really be necessary," he said. "Today, we're just rehearsing the movements of the wedding party. If you insist, though, we can do it again tomorrow with music."

She made a snorting sound. "Okay, music tomorrow. Everything must be perfect for wedding."

Darren Culpepper's shoulders quivered, and as he turned to look at his brother, I could see that he was quietly laughing. Father Dao's face creased in a look of reproof. "Now, at this point, the maid of honor will begin her procession down the aisle." He raised his eyes toward the back.

Constance Liu stood there, wearing white cotton shorts and a pink blouse. At a nod from the priest, she began walking toward the front. Behind her, his face beaming with pride, walked Gordon Liu, in a dark gray suit with a crisply knotted tie, his arm linked in his daughter, Amy's arm. Even though she was wearing a green skirt that stopped at mid-thigh and a rumpled looking mint green blouse, she looked the picture of a blushing bride. There were murmurs of approval from the audience as the trio made their way slowly toward the front. Darren Culpepper watched them approach, a broad smile on his face. His brother, standing at his side, looked bored.

When they reached the stage, Liu helped Amy step up beside Culpepper, who took her hand, gazing down at her with shining eyes. Constance stepped to her sister's left, facing the priest. The couple turned to face the priest.

"At this point," the priest began. "I will begin _ -"

Darren had leaned in toward Amy, but then he stumbled forward, releasing Amy's hand and grasping at his right shoulder with his left hand. He made a grunting sound. I saw a geyser of blood spurt from his right shoulder. Amy, her mouth gaping, suddenly screamed and grabbed for him as he began slumping down.

The priest's face crumpled and his hands flew to his chest. I could see a spreading dark stain on the front of his shirt between the vee-shape of his coat. He fell slowly backwards, knocking over the wire frame arch.

Pandemonium erupted, as people began screaming, shouting, and dropping to the grass, overturning chairs. I grabbed Sandra and shoved her down between the chairs, shielding her body with my own as I tried to make sense of the chaos around us.

My body had reacted reflexively, but my mind was having difficulty processing. The spreading red stain on Darren Culpepper's shoulder, the thick red mass pooling around the priest's inert form; none of this fit with the brilliant blue sky, the fluffy clouds; the sounds of screams and cries, competing with the raucous cries of birds in the nearby trees.

Culpepper had been stunned, but not knocked unconscious. As Amy bent over him, he grabbed her and pulled her down and started pushing her toward the back of the platform, over the body of the priest. Marcus Culpepper still stood at the edge of the platform, looking toward the mountains with a puzzled expression.

My mind clicked into place when a portly man, three rows from the front of the chairs

Charles Ray

across from us, started to rise, and the top of his head exploded in a spray of blood, hair, flesh, and bone. His body collapsed among the chairs like a puppet that has had its strings suddenly cut. When those nearest him felt the sting of body parts and the hot splash of blood from his ruined head, the screaming increased in volume.

But, I knew now what was happening. So did Darren Culpepper. We'd both gone through the same school and had no doubt had similar experiences. We were under fire.

Culpepper had pushed past the dead priest and placed Amy Liu beneath his body to shield her from further fire as he crouched behind the platform. He looked up at his younger brother, still staring toward the mountains. "Marcus," he shouted. "Get your ass down here. Someone's shooting at us."

The younger Culpepper blinked confusedly, and then looked down at his brother. "Uh, huh?"

"Get down, fool."

He shook his head and then dropped behind the platform to crouch near his brother.

I was shielding Sandra as I scanned the area, trying to see if I could determine where the shots were coming from. From the way the first shot had struck Culpepper's shoulder and then struck the priest in the chest, at a lower level, indicated that it been shot from above us. The only place I could see that had a view of the area near the pool, that was elevated, was the mountains, and the nearest ledge looked to be nearly two thousand meters away. I shook my head. A professional sniper, given time to line the shot up, could have done it. The shooter had fired high, probably over compensating for the distance. Not a mistake a trained sniper would make, but whoever he was, he was still good to have hit a target at all from that distance.

My main objective now, though, was to get Sandra and the others out of the line of fire. We were about twenty yards from the reception building. If people stayed near the center of the main dining room, they'd have the bulk of the building between them and the area where I thought the shots must have come from. I looked around. Quincy had dropped to the grass, and worked his way to the front row, where he hovered protectively over Mei Ling Chao. Constance Liu was huddled near them, clutching her arms around her mother's shoulders.

"Listen up, everyone," I shouted. "We've got to get to cover. So, keep low and work your way to the restaurant as quickly as you can."

Some of them had already started in that direction. A few had started to rise, but at the sound of my voice, dropped back to their knees and began crawling toward the building. Except for some sobbing, it was quieter now.

"Darren, Amy," I said. "Are you two okay?"

"I took one through the shoulder," Darren Culpepper's voice came. "But, I can move. Good idea, moving to the building. We'll link up with you there."

I watched as the three of them, Darren, Amy, and Marcus, crouching low, Amy with her arms around Darren's waist, made it to a large clump of bushes behind the stage, and then ran toward the shelter of the reception building.

With my hand on the small of Sandra's back, I guided her past the pool and into a side door of the building. I crouched there, hugging the wall, guiding the rest of the panicked crowd into the building. When I was satisfied that everyone was inside, I slipped in.

Inside the restaurant, everyone was standing around or sitting, dazed looks on their faces.

"W-what's happening?" Gordon Liu asked as I approached him. "Why was someone shooting at us?"

"I don't know, sir," I said. "Right now, our first priority is to notify the police." I looked around for Kono. He was busily directing the wait staff to get coffee, water, or even something stronger for the milling people. I walked over to him. "Did you call the police?"

He looked at me, his face clouded with a stricken look. "I was standing near the building when it started," he said. "I didn't know what was happening at first, but when that guy's head exploded, I knew. Oh, bra, did I know. It was like being back in Iraq all over again. I ran back to my office to call the cops down in Kahului, but the line's dead."

"Don't you have a hand phone, or a radio?"

"Cell phones don't work up here, and I been thinking 'bout buying a shortwave, but just hadn't got 'round to it."

"Damn," I said. "Do you have a car or truck? Maybe we could send someone down for help."

"We have an old pickup, but it's in the shed down past the helipad."

Shit. That would mean crossing over a hundred yards of open ground, in plain view of the shooter. For now, we were pinned down. The shooter had the advantage of high ground, a clear field of fire, and us with nowhere to go. The situation was rapidly pissing me off.

"Well, I guess we might as well try and make everyone comfortable," I said. "We're not going anywhere for a while."

"Then what we gonna do?" Kono asked.

"Then, I'm going out and find the son of a bitch that's shooting at us."

12.

Time dragged. Time shuffled on slipper-clad feet. If you've never been cooped up in a large room with nearly seventy frightened people, you can't possibly understand how it feels. It stinks. Spiritually as well as physically. The 'stench of fear' is not just an overblown literary phrase. It's real. Fear causes adrenalin to surge through the system, triggering the flight or fright reflex, which releases pheromones that have a rank, unpleasant odor, a lot like the odor of stale piss and sour milk.

When it's only one or two people, the smell is hardly noticed, but, a large, panicked crowd in an enclosed space can generate a miasma that is almost overpowering. Like a grass fire, it feeds on itself, setting up a feedback loop with people infecting those nearest them, and, in turn, being re-infected by the fear they themselves have caused.

Despite the best efforts of Kono and his staff, the mood in the restaurant was gloomy, worsened when everyone discovered that cell phones didn't work, and bordering on total pandemonium when they learned that the land line, their last link to civilization and safety, was dead.

Sandra and I joined Kono and the others in trying to calm everyone.

"Listen, folks," I said. "We're all safe in here. It's just a matter of time until someone from town wonders why they can't reach us. Just stay near the center of the room."

Gordon Liu, more composed than the rest, approached me. "What do you think is happening? Why would someone be shooting at us?"

"I wish I knew, sir. Can you think of anyone who might want to hurt you or any members of your family?"

He shrugged and shook his head.

"What about your future son-in-law? How much do you know about him?"

"The Culpeppers have been here in the islands for three generations. His grandfather started the construction business. It was small at first, just small jobs for the military on Oahu. When the old man passed away and Darren's father took over, he expanded to commercial construction, and became a very wealthy man. Darren joined the navy right out of college and only returned here a few months ago, so I can't see how he could have made enemies angry enough to shoot at him in that time."

That was troubling; if it wasn't personal, that meant a random shooter, and that didn't make sense. Serial killers, as far as I knew, didn't usually target remote places like Maui. I kept this to myself, though. There was no sense adding any more to the already growing sense of fear.

I walked over to where they'd put two tables together and laid Darren Culpepper on them to tend his wounds. His shirt had been removed and Quincy, with Sandra's help, had cleaned and bandaged his shoulder. He lay on the tables, pale and in obvious pain, but bearing it stoically, with Amy sitting beside him, her hand on his uninjured shoulder and a worried look on her face.

"How're you feeling?" I asked.

He looked over at me and smiled wanly. "Well, it hurts like hell, but I think I'll live. Did you see where the shots came from?"

"Not exactly see; but, the only place anyone could have shot from concealment looks to be over a thousand meters away."

"Damn, whoever it is has to be a crack shot to hit someone from that distance."

"What I don't understand is, why would anyone want to shoot you?"

His eyes narrowed. "I can think of a few hundred, but most of them are thousands of miles away from here, and I doubt if they'd be able to enter Hawaii without triggering a few alarms."

He didn't need to go into details. I could well imagine that his SEAL team had discomfited more than a few people who needed discomfiting, which left a lot of relatives and shady colleagues thirsting for revenge. But, this didn't have the smell of that kind of operation, which tends to be up close and personal. This was someone shooting from concealment, and as I thought about it, the target seemed clearly to be Culpepper. The second shot, had the unfortunate victim not stood when he did, would have probably hit him.

I was wondering why the shooter had taken as long as he did for that second shot. Something about that time lag was tickling at my mind, but it wouldn't clearly show itself.

"What about since you've been back in Hawaii? Any competitors who'd like to see you out of the picture?"

"Well, the construction business can be pretty cut throat." He laughed, and then winced. "Ow, shouldn't laugh. It hurts. Anyway, the cutthroat competition is figurative. We don't have any mob connections here in Hawaii like they do back east on the mainland. You think I'm the main target?"

"That's what my gut tells me. Of course, having missed, the shooter's at a disadvantage. He now has to come out in the open to get at you."

The shooter had us – me – outgunned. I don't carry a gun, haven't since a few years before I retired from the army except for one time when I had to use one against a rogue FBI agent. If he decided to do some close-in hunting, it would take all my skills to keep Culpepper; or myself; alive.

13.

By five pm some of the panic had subsided, to be replaced by boredom and cabin fever. Now, people were just irritated at being cooped up in a single space. There were a few murmurings of complaint until Kono had the waitresses open the bar. After a few minutes, there was still murmuring, but it was less fervent – almost bearable, as the murmurings of drunks can sometimes be at that point in a party when people are just beginning to feel the effects of the alcohol, believing they're high, and before the depressive effects hit them. A few were even smiling and laughing, their panic of just moments before relegated to some dark recess of their minds.

I was standing near the door leading into the reception desk when I heard the grinding of gears and rumbling of what sounded like a four-wheel-drive vehicle. I walked through the reception area, followed by Kono and Quincy. I stopped at the main entrance, looking out. The mountains were off to the right, the south slope of the south peak just visible at the edge of the building. Figuring I was out of the line of fire of our invisible sniper, I walked outside and stood under the concrete awning.

I could see a jeep just coming over the last rise in the winding road from the base of the hill. There was one person in it. As it got closer, I could see that it looked like an old army surplus jeep with canvas sides and top, but it had been painted blue and there was a colorful looking crest on the right door, 'Wailuku Sheriff's Department.' A whip antenna was swaying from the back bumper.

The jeep circled the entrance drive and came to a shuddering halt. The engine made little whining and pinging sounds as the ignition was turned off. A tall young Hawaiian, wearing green pants, a green shirt, a light green jacket with yellow sergeant's stripes and brown baseball cap got out and came toward us. He had a gold badge over his left breast and a .45 caliber automatic in a black leather holster on his right hip.

"Jason, bruddah," Kono called to him as he

approached. "Man, are we glad to see you."

The man had a broad face, bronze colored like most Hawaiians, dark brown eyes, and a straight nose with a bump midway up that looked like it had been broken once and badly reset. He looked to be about Kono's age, perhaps in his early thirties. His smile was broad, but his eyes scanned Quincy and me with practiced efficiency.

"Hey, Kono," he said. "Looks like you got quite a crowd up here. How's business?"

Looking back over my shoulder, I saw that several people had crowded in the door between the restaurant and reception.

Kono greeted the visitor with a hand slap and a hug. "Bra, I got a full house, but we got trouble like you ain't gonna believe. First, though, let me introduce you to two of my guests."

As he introduced us, we shook hands. His grip was strong. "Folks, this is Jason Kaheamui; he's the main law down in Wailuku."

"Pleased to meet you," Kaheamui said. Turning back to Kono, he said, "What's the problem that Xanadu needs a cop?"

Kono turned to me. "Maybe you should explain it since you were right there when it happened."

I gave him as detailed an account of the morning's events as possible. When I'd finished, his smile had turned to a serious, professional expression. "Show me the bodies," he said.

"Okay, but we'd be out in the open, and I'm not sure the shooter's not still watching us."

"Maybe if we stay against the side of the building, he won't see us." But, there was no conviction in his voice. "Then again, maybe I should get back down to town and call Honolulu and ask them to send the state police. You say you got a wounded man, too?"

"Yes," I said. "You better have them send a doctor, too."

"We patched him up as best we could," Quincy said. "But, a doctor really oughta look at his injury."

"Why didn't you call when it happened?" he asked Kono.

"Tried, bra, but the land line is dead, and you know cell phones don't work up here."

"Hell of a place to put a hotel," Kaheamui said. "I lost radio contact halfway up the road. Can't even call from here. Look, I don't like leaving you folks up here alone with somebody out there gunning for you. Tell you what; I'll go back down the road till I can get radio contact and call for backup, then I'll come back."

Our three heads nodded. At that moment, it was not just the best solution to our problems – it was the only solution.

He turned and started toward his jeep. Quincy and I followed. When he was about six feet from the vehicle, the left front tire exploded. There was a pinging sound of something striking metal. He pulled his .45, looking right toward the mountain. From where we were standing, both peaks were now visible. That meant we were visible as well. About five seconds later, there was a popping and pinging sound from the right side of the vehicle and the hood canted downward, and after another five seconds, the there was a loud pinging sound and a geyser of steam billowed from beneath the jeep's hood. Pieces of blue metal flew off the front of the vehicle, scything through the air toward us. Kaheamui and I both dove for the ground, inching back toward the building.

I heard Quincy make a grunting sound as he fell to his knees, grabbing at his chest. I stopped my backward movement and crawled quickly to his side. He knelt there, a stricken look on his face, with a triangular shape stuck in his chest. Blood was welling up around it, staining his shirt dark.

"Ow," he said. "That hurts."

Charles Ray

14.

With Kaheamui's help I got Quincy back inside the reception area. I gingerly removed the piece of shrapnel. The wound was deep and bled freely, but didn't look fatal, but he'd lost blood and was looking pale. One of the waitresses brought the first aid kit and after stripping off his shirt, we got the bleeding stopped and bandaged it.

Two more tables were pulled together, and Quincy joined Darren Culpepper in our makeshift hospital in the restaurant.

Kaheamui and I went back to reception. We looked out at his ruined jeep.

"Shit," he said. "I just got that damn thing tuned up. The town council's gonna have puppies when I ask them to buy me a new one."

I had to laugh at his priorities. Here we were trapped inside the building with a gunman out there able to pick us off if we dared show our heads, and he was worried about the feelings of a bunch of politicians.

"Right now, that's the least of our worries. The way I see it, we're trapped here. We can't get out. We can't call for help. That son of a bitch, whoever he is, is holding all the cards."

"This is kinda like the puzzles they threw at us during ranger training," he said. "Supposed to be impossible situations, and we'd be so tired we couldn't think straight anyway. I always found a way out of 'em, though."

"So, you were an army ranger?" I asked.

"Yeah, for four years. I was with the rangers when we kicked the Iraqis' asses out of Kuwait. After my hitch, I decided I'd had enough of the big wide world, so I came back home. They made me sheriff 'cause nobody else wanted the job."

"Well, do you remember anything from your ranger days that might help us get out of this mess?"

His eyes narrowed in concentration. "Not really," he said finally. "There's no way we're getting out of here as long as there's light. I suppose we could wait until dark and try to use the spa's pickup."

"That might work assuming whoever is doing the shooting doesn't have night vision goggles."

He laughed. "You're just a bundle of optimism, aren't you? We don't really have much choice, though, unless you're suggesting we hunker down here until someone down below gets curious, or we run out of food."

"Speaking of food, maybe we should eat while we wait for darkness."

He didn't argue with me on that. We went into the restaurant, which was quieter now, with people sitting around in small groups nursing hangovers and looking gloomy. Sandra, Constance, and Mei Ling were hovering over Quincy who still looked a bit pale, but seemed to be resting comfortably. Amy hadn't moved from Darren's side. He, too, was pale, but was sleeping, occasionally twitching or tossing under a table cloth that someone had put over his body.

We found an empty table near the large windows overlooking the helipad. A waitress came and took our orders. From the amount of food he ordered, Kaheamui obviously hadn't eaten since lunch. Like me, though, he ordered water to wash his food down. I knew, without asking, what he was thinking: we would need all our faculties to avoid becoming the sniper's next victims.

We ate in silence and watched the

lengthening shadows outside. We were nearly finished when Sandra joined us. "You two are awful quiet," she said. "And, if I know you, Al Pennyback, it means you're planning something." She smiled at Kaheamui, who introduced himself around a mouthful of the steak he was demolishing.

I kept my voice low as I explained what we planned to do.

"Isn't that dangerous?" she asked, her eyes wide. "I mean, all you have is that one little pistol." She looked down at the automatic on Kaheamui's hip.

"This wouldn't do us much good against someone shooting from up on the mountain," he said. "Not enough range. You should have seen what it did to my jeep. That guy has some firepower up there. No, we'll be using the cover of darkness."

His words tripped a switch in my mind. "You know, something's been eating at me. The slugs that hit your jeep had to be pretty big to do the damage they did. In addition, the one that hit Darren Culpepper went through and through and still had enough power to kill the priest, and the second slug nearly disintegrated the top of the second victim's skull."

"Sounds like maybe a .50 caliber," he said. "That's about the only thing that packs that much punch from the range you estimated."

"Yeah, and the time between shots; like he was taking time to reload."

"Damn, uh, excuse me ma'am," he said. "He's got a sniper rifle. Sounds like the single shot version." He shook his head and smiled wryly. "I guess we're lucky he doesn't have one of the new ones with the five-round magazine."

"Are you thinking what I'm thinking?" I asked.

"I don't think I like where this is going," Sandra said.

I didn't either, but it made sense. It was, in fact, probably our only chance if we were unable to get out in the pickup.

"Yeah," I said. "You and me are gonna have to go hunting."

"Just like ranger training," he said.

Sandra stood up, a look of exasperation on her face. "My God, it's bad enough I have to deal with you, Al. Now I have two of you."

She stomped off, returning to Quincy's side.

"I think your lady's upset," Kaheamui said.

Charles Ray

15.

We waited until it was fully dark outside; Jason Kaheamui and I; and with Sandra glaring at us, made our way to the front entrance.

Easing out the door, we made our way left, hugging the wall of the building. It was dark, but we decided it best to take no chances.

"You know, sheriff," I said in a quiet voice. "You never did say why you came up here. We weren't able to call for help."

He was close behind me. I could feel the heat from his body. "Oh, there was a chopper from Kahului that didn't come back yesterday," he said, just as quietly. "They got cops scouring the island for it. I figure he might have had engine problems and had to land somewhere.

Worse case is he hit a patch of cloud and clipped a tree. I cover this part of the island from Wailuku, so I thought I'd start up here is all. Hell, if I'd known what was happening here, I'd of called the state police and brought a SWAT team with me. And, just call me Jason, Mr. Pennyback."

"Okay, Jason. I'm Al. I guess if we're about to get shot together, we might as well die as friends."

He chuckled. "Like I said; you're just a bundle of optimism."

As we reached the edge of the building, we hunched over and ran in a zig zag pattern past the helipad, angling toward the squat metal roofed building set in a clearing behind one of the cabanas.

I could feel a tingling between my shoulder blades as we ran. If the shooter had night vision goggles, while he wouldn't have a really clear shot at us, we'd be in the open for the last ten feet, and he might get lucky.

The tingling didn't stop until we reached the front of the maintenance shed. The metal door in the center of the front wall was slightly ajar. We quickly slipped inside and I closed the door. Jason felt around beside the door for the light switch. Two yellow bulbs, suspended from the cross beams of the metal roof, bathed the room in an amber glow.

A rusty, blue pickup, with the hood up, sat in the center. Jason walked over and peered under the hood. "Shit," he said.

When I joined him, I saw what had caused his expletive. Someone had ripped the distributor cap from its base and cut the cords. Little worms of black leather tubing lay on top of the engine. Whoever had sabotaged the vehicle hadn't even bothered to remove the large grass shear they'd used. They lay on top of the engine as well.

"Shit is right," I said. "I'm guessing there's not a spare distributor lying around."

Just to be sure, we searched the shed. Among the untidy piles of junk, there was indeed no distributor.

"Well, so much for driving for help," Jason said. "What do we do now?"

That was a good question, one to which we both knew the answer. But, it was, I suppose, left to me to say it aloud.

"We're going hunting."

Charles Ray

16.

We made our way back to the reception building, back to the restaurant, where now the tables, except for the four being used as makeshift hospital beds for Quincy and Darren, were moved against the walls, and the staff had scoured the linen closets for table cloths that had been folded and pressed into service as cots and pillows. The place looked like a high school gymnasium after a tornado, with people lying in groups of two or more, scattered about the room. The lights had been turned out. A few were already asleep; the raspy sound of snoring coming from several places. Others lay staring up at the ceiling. A few swiveled their heads to track our progress as we made our way to where Sandra sat, a table cloth draped over her knees, her back against one of the tables upon which Quincy lay, still pale, but sleeping.

I knelt beside Sandra and whispered to her. "The truck's inoperative, babe."

"So, we're trapped here," she whispered. "I guess I know what that means."

"No choice. We can't just sit here until this son of bitch picks us off one by one."

"Dammit," she whispered hoarsely. "I know that, but, why does it always have to be you?"

"Because, I'm the only one who can. Jason's going with me. He's a former ranger, so the two of us have a chance."

She pulled my head down into the crook of her neck. I could feel her body trembling. I felt the warmth of tears coating her cheeks. "Al Pennyback, you'd better come back, you hear. I'll never forgive you if you get yourself killed."

There was so much I wanted to say to her, but the words wouldn't come. I put my arms around her, rubbing her back as I pulled her against me. "I wouldn't like it too much either if I got killed," was all I could say. Look, you get some sleep. I've got to talk to Jason before we leave."

She pulled my head around and kissed me, deeply, longingly, letting our lips and tongues say what words couldn't. I knew what was in her heart, and she knew what was in mine. Words weren't necessary.

She released me and folded the tablecloth, laying it out parallel to the table, and lay back, her eyes closed. In the glow of the moonlight filtering through the uncurtained windows, I could see the glisten of her tear stained cheeks.

I rose and went back to Jason, who was standing gazing out the window at the dark, and now forbidding looking landscape beyond the boundaries of the resort. What by day had looked so idyllic and peaceful was about to become a battleground.

"What time should we leave?" he asked.

"I figure he can't stay awake all night. He'll figure we'll try to sleep, so he might as well too. We need to get to the cover of the forest well before light."

"It's about a thousand meters to the first heavy brush and trees. Take us about ten minutes if we move fast, about twenty if we use stealth."

"When's first light?"

"Out here, about three in the morning it's light enough to see."

"Okay, let's figure twenty minutes from here to cover. We need to be concealed before he can see – assuming he's not awake and using night goggles – so, we need to take off around one."

"Sounds like a plan."

I looked at my watch. It was half past nine. "We might as well get some rest."

He walked over and pulled a chair near the window, sitting there staring out into the darkness. I straddled a chair and watched Sandra sleep. Except for Jason and me, everyone was asleep. The darkness, despite the dim glow of a sliver of moon outside, was heavy, closing around me like a thick fog, and pressing against my skin. The quiet, punctuated periodically by a gasped snore, or someone moaning quietly, was oppressive.

I glanced frequently at my watch, the green numerals pulsing in the darkness, watching the minutes flip by.

The sound of a chair scratching the floor jerked me from my reverie. I turned to see Jason straddling a chair next to me.

"You can't sleep either," he said. "This reminds me of Iraq just before a mission."

"Yeah, the waiting's the hardest part."

I looked at my watch again. It was 10:59. I'd been sitting there, unaware of the passage of time despite looking at the watch.

"So," he said. "How do you think we should do this?"

I was on unfamiliar territory. The main thing was to make it into the forest without being spotted. After that, it would be a game of cat and mouse as we tried to locate the sniper; hopefully, before he located us.

"Once we make it to the cover of the trees, I'll have to follow your lead."

"Hell, I haven't been up in those mountains for a while. If this guy's found a good hidey hole, it won't be easy to sneak up on him."

"I thought you rangers were supposed to be expert trackers."

"Naw, that's you sneaky-Petes. We worked in platoon sized formations. It was you guys who skulked around the jungle alone."

"Not if I could help it. Smallest unit I operated with was a ten-man team."

I would have given almost anything to have my old team, the Wolverines, with me right then, backed up by a flight of A-10 fighters and a few Blackhawks. But, at least Jason had ranger training, which was better than going into the mountains with an untrained person, or alone.

I hadn't been in a situation like this since leaving the army; even before leaving, actually, since my last couple of years in uniform had been in a Pentagon assignment, where the toughest mission was getting the general's coffee to him before it got cold. I stay in shape through jogging, my martial arts exercises, and meditation, so I was feeling confident that I could handle it physically. Mentally; well, once you've had combat experience, it's sort of stuck in your mind. Like riding a bicycle, you might get rusty, but you never forget.

The wry expression on Jason Kaheamui's face led me to the conclusion that he was thinking along the same lines.

"Well," he said. "We don't have my ranger platoon, and we don't have you're A Team, so we'll just have to be smarter, faster, and tougher than our sniper."

"I'd feel a lot more comfortable if you had a bit more firepower, but if the two of us can't get this guy, - -"

"Hey, stop with the pessimism. We'll get him."

17.

We slipped out the front door just before one am. We worked our way slowly to the left, down past the helipad, and then cut across to the road. It didn't give us perfect cover, especially if the sniper had night vision goggles, but it increased our chances of remaining unseen.

Working our way along the road, we kept to the bushes that grew up nearly to the poles from which the phone line hung, bending over so as not to present silhouettes against the sky. We were a hundred yards from the reception building when I heard Jason, who had been a few feet in front of me, curse. When I caught up to him and looked up to where he was looking, I saw the reason.

Someone, probably our sniper, had cut the

phone lines, leaving the wire hanging limply against the poles. Neither wire reached the ground, indicating that whoever had cut them had removed a section to make it impossible for us to splice them back together. First the damaged car, now the cut phone lines. This guy was good. He'd effectively cut us off from outside help, and had it not been for Jason coming to look for the missing helicopter, we'd still be sitting ducks. Oh, I might have to come to the conclusion to go after him on my own, but I knew that unarmed, against a killer armed with a .50 caliber weapon, even a single shot weapon, my chances would have been slim. They weren't all that good for the two of us – just not as bad.

"This bastard's beginning to really piss me off," he said.

We darted across the road, and immediately began an uphill climb. For the first ten yards or so, it was relatively open ground, with just a few clumps of vegetation scattered about, but, we quickly came to thicker trees. A short walk into the trees, and it was as if someone had drawn a curtain. The darkness closed in on us like a giant's hand, with only faint slivers of silver and gold from moonlight that penetrated the few spaces in the canopy over us. I couldn't see it, but I could also feel the mist closing in on us as we went higher. The moisture in the air caused my shirt to cling to my body, and the damp crotch of my pants made walking uncomfortable.

After about five minutes walking, Jason stopped and held up his hand.

"I think this is far enough in," he whispered as I came abreast of him. "We need to find a dry place to hold up until first light."

He was right. We had no chance of seeing him in the dark, and every chance of stumbling into his line of sight and getting our asses blown off. Where, though, were we to find a dry place? Jason did know the mountain and the forest. He found a little hummock, surrounded by gnarled trees that, though moist, felt dry in comparison to what we'd been enduring. We climbed on top and sat back to back. We'd been walking for just over an hour. It was now two am; two hours until the sky would start to lighten and light would start to penetrate the thick tree cover.

"Why don't you grab an hour's shuteye," I said. "Then, I'll wake you and you can watch while I nap."

I could feel the movement of his head bobbing up and down, and then, just the regular expansion and contraction of his upper body as he breathed. Yup, he was a ranger all right. Those guys can go to sleep standing waist deep in a creek. He couldn't sleep in the building before starting out, but, now that the mission was underway his body was in recon mode. I knew, also, that when I tapped him when it was his time to keep watch, he'd be awake and alert in an instant.

I let my body and mind relax, going into a meditation mode. Contrary to popular belief, this isn't a trance state. When I'm in a proper meditation, all of my senses are heightened. I see, hear, feel, taste, *sense*, more than would ever be possible under normal circumstances. The sounds of the surrounding jungle; the raucous call of night birds, the croak of frogs, and a far-off grunting sound that I couldn't identify, were clear without being intrusive. The sweet smell of flowers and an exotic odor, which I finally realized was sandalwood, drifted gently up my nose. I could feel the tendrils of a soft breeze that was barely enough to stir the leaves.

So many times I'd been in a situation like this. Holing up in a night position before moving on to the final objective, my back against the back of the man who'd trudged through the jungle, mountain, forest, or desert with me, feeling the heat of his body, sensing the tension of his muscles.

It was like old times.

18.

I looked down at the faint green glow of my watch face. *2:59*. Then the little rectangle blinked: *3:00*. I was tempted to let Jason sleep, which I knew was a mistake. Even an hour of shut eye could make the difference between being alert or letting your attention stray, and that could get you killed.

Before I could reach around and tap his shoulder, I felt his back tense, and then he leaned forward and stretched. The habits of someone who'd had lots of experience on long night patrols. You sleep when you can, your mind and body programmed for a certain duration. You wake up, alert and ready for duty. Or, you don't develop the ability, and you die. He was still alive. The kid was good.

"Okay," he whispered. "Your turn. I'll wake you at oh four hundred."

He was even slipping back into the lingo.

I relaxed and let my head slump forward, asleep before I felt my chin hit my chest. And, it seemed like a moment later, my eyes snapped open. Glancing down at my watch, I saw that it was 3:59. I hadn't lost the ability either.

I stretched and stepped off the hummock. Jason followed. He wandered off into the bushes ringing the little hill, and I heard the splash as he relieved himself. When he returned, zipping his trousers, I took my turn.

"Man, I could sure use a cup of coffee right now," he said.

"What we need is water. Even with all the moisture in the air, we could get dehydrated after a few hours walking through this stuff."

"Water's no problem. Lots of streams up here, and the water's as pure as you've ever seen. Ain't much to eat, though."

The sky, or what we could see of it through the little triangles of space between the gray-green foliage overhead, was light gray with tinges of orange. The air was still damp. The morning sounds of birds and other creatures was a symphony, coming at us from all directions.

"Okay, Daniel Boone," I said. "Let's find some water. Then we can decide how we want to look for this guy."

He started uphill, brushing aside the palm fronds and bushes without making noise, and scanning all around as he walked. I let him get about ten feet ahead of me, and then followed.

I heard the burbling sound of the water ahead of us. We came around a tree with its mottled and gnarled limbs covered with reddish-brown lichen, half its roots anchored in a three-foot wide stream that flowed over black polished rocks. He knelt at the edge, his knees making an indentation in the moss-covered bank, and cupping his hands, scooped water into his mouth. I knelt beside him and did the same. The water was crystal clear, cold, and refreshing as it slid down my throat.

After slaking my thirst, I dashed a handful of the cold water over my face. Not that I needed it to wake up. All my senses were alert, but the sting of the cold water on my stubbled cheeks felt good.

We knelt side by side, him looking to the front and right, me covering the left and rear.

"Here's how I think we should do this," he said. His proposal was that we work our way north, up the slope, until we thought we were above where the gunman might be shooting from, and then cutting east, we'd be able to come at him – hopefully – from a direction he wouldn't be anticipating. It was a long shot, but, it was better than anything I could come up with. Besides, Jason knew the terrain, and I didn't, so I agreed.

We followed the stream uphill for a ways until its course turned west. As we walked, Jason quietly pointed out and named geographic features, trees, animals, and birds, proud of the fact that he knew most of them. We were climbing Puu Kukui, he said, or West Maui Mountain. Once reaching a height of 8,000 feet, time has eroded it, until it's but a remnant of its original self, and carved a notch in it, giving it the appearance of two mountains. The western end of Maui is the wettest part of the island, getting as much as 400 inches of rain a year, and almost continuous moisture from the clouds that hang over the eroded peak of Puu Kukui.

There were shelves terraced along the slopes, carved out by centuries of wind and water, some large enough to serve as a landing site for small and medium helicopters. I noticed that as we climbed, Jason paid particular attention to each ledge.

But for the deadly nature of our mission, I could have enjoyed the trek; the plunging waterfalls that suddenly appeared as you came around a rock ledge, grottoes of opalesque ferns, lush and undisturbed, brilliantly colored birds and strange looking aquatic creatures in the crystalline streams that cut across the face of the mountain like a network of spider webs. The whistles, squeaks, croaks, and groans of birds and frogs, occasionally startled into silence by grunts that Jason said was from the wild hogs that infested the island. A species not native to Maui, the pigs had been introduced by early farmers, had escaped and thrived in the wild, and was now threatening the ecological balance through its destruction of plants and watersheds. With man being its only predator, it was on the verge of outnumbering the human population and bankrupting the tourism industry.

"I know you might have heard of Hawaiian luaus and roast pig," he said. "Because the *only* good pig is a dead pig."

He assured me that the long-snouted porkers posed no physical danger to us, but I kept a wary eye out anyway. Even farm-bred pigs will attack if threatened, and boars, with their razor sharp tusks, can rip your guts out if they knock you down and hook you just right.

We paced ourselves, so by mid-day, we figured we were still an hour away from the point where we'd start working our way east and back down. We were in an area that sloped only slightly, looked in fact to be leveling out, with trees scattered so as to give us more view of the sky than we'd seen all day. Jason, about ten feet ahead of me, suddenly stopped, staring straight ahead.

As I came abreast of him, he pointed. I could see a glint of light, sunlight reflecting off a metal surface, about a hundred yards ahead. Slowly, cautiously, we inched forward. As we came to the edge of the tree line, we looked out on a broad, flat area, some two hundred yards by two hundred yards, a large square with little vegetation. A perfect landing zone, and sitting in the middle was a small, bubble canopied helicopter. It looked like the one I'd seen fly over the spa.

Jason drew his weapon and started slowly forward. I followed, keeping an eye on our rear.

A figure sat in the right front seat. As we neared, I could see that the head was at an odd angle. Closer, the open, sightless eyes, and the grimace of pain on the mouth told the story. The young pilot's neck had been snapped as he sat strapped into the pilot's seat. He probably died before he knew what was happening.

We examined the area in a circle around the aircraft out to the edge of the ledge, where it dropped off to a narrow valley over a hundred feet below. Crushed grass to the northeast indicated that someone had passed this way. I knew, then, how the sniper had gotten above us. It also told me that we were dealing with a calculating, stone cold killer.

Jason's face was contorted with anger.

"Did you know him?" I asked.

"I met him a few times. Nice guy; wife and two kids. He didn't deserve this."

I pointed in the direction of the crushed grass. "Looks like our quarry headed where I thought. It's unlikely he'll be expecting anyone from up here, so that might enable us to surprise him. How long do you think it is from here to a place from which he could get a shot at the spa?"

"Well, he'd have to be within two thousand yards." He squinted toward the southeast. "I figure an hour, hour and a half from here."

"Okay," I said. "We need to approach carefully. You have the only weapon, so I think I should take the lead."

"Huh?" Then he realized what I'd meant. "You plan to use yourself as bait?"

I nodded. "So, don't miss, kid."

Charles Ray

19.

We set off, with me in front breaking trail; Jason followed, about fifteen yards behind me, but off the trail, concealed in the bushes. The kid was good. I'd look back over my shoulder every few minutes, but there wasn't a trace of his presence, no crackling of footsteps on the undergrowth, not a single movement of the foliage to mark his passage. The rangers had taught him well.

The terrain, level at first, rose up more sharply as the morning went on, and I found myself working my way up steep, rugged slopes covered with trees with swollen trunks and gnarled roots clinging to the rocky ground. Like the trees we'd encountered earlier, these were covered with lichen that was more rust-colored than orange, though, with flowers the color of fresh cut salmon steaks. As I reached the top of the slope, on relatively even ground, the trees had the same blue-gray gnarled trunks, but the blossoms were bright red. Looking closer, I could see that the trunks differed as well, with vertical striations of color ranging from blue-gray to white.

I walked out in the open, or as much in the open as one can be in a rain forest. A broad path between the trees, covered in a thick carpet grayish-green moss that hugged the black earth. To either side, in among the trees, large ferns, some towering over me, spread their branches as if in prayer. Down through the few slits in the blue-brown-gray-green ceiling over me, the sun's rays filtered through in dazzling rays of silver and gold, tinged with green.

While I was in relatively good shape, having not eaten since the day before, and having to navigate some of the most demanding terrain I'd encountered in a long time was beginning to take its toll. I wasn't exactly gasping for breath, but I was sucking hard to pull air into my nostrils, and exhaling through my mouth, I could hear the ragged out-gush of air. My thighs were burning, and I could feel the muscles of my calves tightening.

I figured Jason was doing a little better. He was, after all, a lot younger. But, if we didn't find the sniper soon, we'd both be too tired to walk, much less fight him.

The trail I followed was clear, a space about three feet wide where there was nothing but the soft moss beneath my feet. In a few places, I could see where the moss had been torn away, revealing the scarred black earth beneath. I remembered Jason telling me about the wild hogs that roamed freely through the forests, rooting for food and basically upsetting the ecological balance. Signs of cloven hoof prints in the soft soil confirmed what had caused the damage I was seeing, but the little clods of dirt that had been casually tossed aside were dry and graying, indicating that it had been done some time ago. The chirping, raucous quacking, and hooting of birds in the dense foliage to my right and left also told me that, except for me, and Jason somewhere in the brush behind me and to my left, there were no other predators in close range.

I pushed on. On ground that was tilting slightly downwards, my breathing slowed. But, my calves still tingled.

I peered ahead, and to right and left, alert, I thought, to any movement that might indicate something in the bush that shouldn't be there. So intent I was on looking for movement, I let my attention wander, and forgot to listen for sounds. It took me a few seconds to register that I was no longer hearing anything but the soft hum of the slight wind through the foliage overhead, a whispering sound like water falling over a ledge. It took a few more seconds for my brain to process what I *wasn't* hearing. The bird calls had stopped.

I slowed my forward progress even more, inching ahead carefully, every sense alert.

The trail ahead curved to the right around the trunk of a large misshapen tree whose roots crawled across the trail like a large gray snake.

Slowly, I approached the tree. Holding my breath, I walked around the side of the tree, hugging that side of the trail.

He stood there. About ten feet away, in the middle of the trail, glaring at me. I put him at about six-one, broad shouldered, with bulging muscles that had to have come from many yours in a gym with heavy weights. The ropy muscles of his thighs bulged beneath the dirt-stained khaki pants he wore. They were darker at the knees, and there were dark stains above his thighs, indicating that he'd been lying on the wet ground, much as a sniper would while taking aim at his target. He wore a white T-shirt that was also stained in front as if he'd lain on the ground for some time and not cleaned away anything but the loose dirt. That he was the sniper we sought was further reinforced by the ugly looking weapon he held casually across his muscled chest. I recognized the harsh lines and lethal appearance of the .50 caliber sniper rifle, its long barrel with the oversized sight on front, and the heavy stock and butt plate. It didn't have a magazine, confirming for me that it was indeed a single shot weapon, but I had no doubts that he had a round in the chamber. A long-bladed knife hung in a leather sheath against his left hip.

His dusty brown hair was cropped close, very short on the sides, military style. He had a broad forehead, encircled by a red bandanna. His eyebrows were light brown, almost invisible against his sun-burnished skin. His age was hard to determine, but I figured he was in his late twenties or early thirties. Hard, mean, brown eyes, like polished marbles, and just as lifeless, regarded me almost negligently. His thin lips, crusted and chapped, were set in a straight line. A muscle in his left cheek twitched.

"Who the fuck are you?" he asked in a raspy voice. "And, what the fuck are you doing up here?"

Charles Ray

20.

I took a slow, deep breath to steady my nerves. No matter how many times you come face to face with someone with a gun, your body tends to react in the same way. It pumps out adrenalin and triggers the fight or flight response. Your muscles tense and your heart starts to beat fast like a jack hammer. Your mouth gets dry and your tongue feels like it's stuck to the roof of your mouth.

The next few seconds, I knew, would mean the difference in my living or dying.

Holding my hands out to my side, I let my mouth drop open in what I hope would look like a combination of shock and surprise. "Oh, I thought you might be part of my group," I said.

Then, I let the words tumble out. "I was out hiking with a group from down in the town, and I went off to get a closer look at some funny looking bird. I guess they didn't notice I was gone, 'cause when I turned back, they were gone. I been wandering around for a couple hours trying to find 'em, but they musta gone back down the mountain to the bus. You know the way out of here?"

I hoped my mumbling tourist act was working, but I couldn't be sure. His eyes narrowed suspiciously, but the weapon remained slanted across his chest. He held it as if it weighed no more than a .22 caliber rifle.

"I ain't heard no busses up here," he said. "And, far as I know, they can't get up this far, 'cause there ain't no roads."

"There's a road that comes around the base of the mountain. We parked and walked up from the road." I looked around, trying to put a look of confusion on my face. All I wanted to do was hold his attention long enough for Jason to get in position for a clear shot, and, I was hoping that Jason hadn't fallen too far behind me. "Uh, I been walking for hours. I musta gone 'round in circles. Ain't no tellin' how far I am from where we come up the mountain. Say, you wouldn't by any chance have any water, would you. I'm parched."

He glanced down at his hip. "Naw, I ain't got

no water with me. Why the hell you out walkin' in these mountains without water?"

The muscle in his cheek was twitching faster now. I could see the whitening of his knuckles as he gripped the .50 caliber harder. Damn, Jason, I thought, you'd better be where you're supposed to be.

"The guide had a canteen," I said, continuing to play the lost tourist. "We weren't supposed to be up here but a few hours."

I began to edge back slowly until I felt my right shoulder brush against the tree. He took a step forward, the barrel of the sniper rifle angling down and around. His lips turned down in a snarl.

"Now, why is it, friend that I find your story a little hard to swallow?" His voice dripped with menace.

I felt a hollow feeling in the pit of my stomach.

"Why is it, I think you're up here looking for something, and it ain't birds?"

"No, no, really," I said. "I was up here with a group, and we were just enjoying the birds and the rain forest."

"Now, that might be true, and it might not. Unfortunately, my friend, you come lookin' in the wrong place."

"I d-don't understand," I said, holding my hands up pleadingly. "I was just bird watching, honest."

Maybe I'm a lousy actor. Maybe there was something in my tone of voice that just wasn't scared enough – although, I was plenty scared; who wouldn't be, standing there unarmed with a goon holding a weapon that could punch a hole through you like a hot knife going through butter – but, it was clear that he wasn't buying. The weapon had almost completed its arc toward me.

"Well, that's just too bad, ain't it," he said. "You know, I always wondered what this thing would do to a target up close."

As he brought the weapon up, the stock against his shoulder, the barrel almost aimed at me, I tensed to jump behind the tree.

What happened next only took a few seconds, but seemed to happen in slow motion – picture and sound, blurred. There were three loud bangs from my left and above me: *Bang! Bang! Bang!* The man in front of me, his arms still tensed as he swung the ugly, menacing black barrel of the sniper rifle in my direction, twitched. His lips turned down in a grimace, and his eyes widened in a look of surprise. Three rosebud-shaped, red spots blossomed on his dirty T-shirt, between his well-developed pectorals. The blossoms were arranged in a rough triangle that I could have covered with my hand, and they were growing, spreading toward each other. The barrel continued in my direction. The surprised look in his eyes was beginning to fade, and his eyes were glazing over. I continued to move for the shelter of the tree trunk, but in my mind, I knew the muzzle velocity of the rifle would send the steel jacketed slug through that tree trunk as if it was no more than a roll of toilet paper, punching through with enough speed and energy left to plow through me as well, but I still dove for cover. The 'flight' reflex was in full control.

I heard the *Boom* of the sniper rifle. He must have managed in a dying reflex to contract his finger. But, he hadn't quite gotten the rifle around far enough. The slug grazed the side of the trunk, gouging out splinters of wood, and whistled off into the jungle. I eased around and peered around the trunk.

The sniper lay, sprawled on his back, four feet from where I'd seen him standing, his right hand still clutching the rifle. The sound of bushes rustling to my left drew my attention. Jason Kaheamui stood, holding his .45 automatic before him in a firing position, his eyes wide.

"Son of a bitch," he said. "The kick on that rifle is something. It picked him up and tossed him back like he was a rag doll."

He made his way down the slight incline to where I stood, shaking my head to clear my hearing which had been somewhat ravaged by the sonic echoes of the shooting.

"That was some good shooting," I said, when the ringing in my ears had subsided to the level of the bells at Canterbury. "Nice tight shot group."

"Thanks for keeping him distracted. Of course, he was one big bastard, so he wasn't hard to hit."

His eyes shone with excitement, and his breathing was shallow as he gazed at the corpse sprawled on the trail, the blood from the three chest shots now a large dark stain across its chest. This was his first time killing a man, and his brain was processing it. I knew the feeling.

"Thanks for shooting when you did. Another second and he would have drilled me right through that tree." I laughed.

That broke the tension. He laughed as well.

"I imagine he has a camp site somewhere around here," he said. "Wonder if he has any food? My stomach is starting to slap my ribs around."

The kid was going to be just fine.

21.

Not forgetting that he was a cop, Jason insisted that we take the sniper's body with us as we moved toward where we suspected he'd been camping. Each of us took hold of an ankle, and, Jason carried the sniper rifle, and we drug him along the trail until we came to an opening on a ledge that had a wide view of the valley below.

I'd objected at first, but Jason said he had a duty to get the corpse down to town so it could be identified, and besides, even this dirt bag, who would have killed us both and left us to rot, couldn't be left for the hogs to get at.

"Damn porkers would leave nothing but the skull, if that," he said. "You know pigs will even eat their young if they're hungry enough."

I shuddered ta the thought, remembering my days as a kid in rural East Texas. I'd heard stories of hogs getting at the corpses of people who'd gotten lost and died in the swamps. They left nothing much to bury, according to the old folks who'd lived in the area for generations. But, I knew Jason was right, and if we could ID the gunman, maybe we could find out why he was using the spa's guests for target practice.

His camp site was set back from the edge of the ledge. A canvas tent was anchored to some small trees, and a ten gallon canvas bag containing tepid water hung from the branches of a larger tree nearby. He'd pushed up dirt to build a firing platform at the very edge of the ledge, and from there, we could see down a relatively gentle slope all the way to the spa. The central building blocked the view of the helipad, but the swimming pool, and the area that had been set aside for the wedding ceremony were in plain sight. I estimated the distance to be just under two thousand yards. A long shot, but one that an experienced sniper could make – had, in fact, made.

We dragged the body over near the tent, and I looked inside. There, on top of a military sleeping bag was an opened box of army rations, the Meals-Ready-to-Eat, or MREs, that GIs take with them on field operations. Two of the cardboard containers of rations were missing, leaving ten full meals.

At the sight of the rations, my stomach started growling. We looked at each other, and then, ignoring the dead man, we pawed through the case, looking for food like the hungry fools we were. Jason took the meat loaf, while I found a box containing franks and beans. The little box with tiny bottles of tabasco sauce, with two bottles missing, was there, and we used a bottle each to add some flavor to the cardboard taste of the cold food, eating even the congealed lumps of fat that clung to the meat. After twenty years in the army, I'd never developed a liking for field rations, but it was the best meal I'd eaten in days.

Once our bellies were full, we set about planning our trip back to the spa.

Since we had decided we'd take the body with us, Jason suggested, and I concurred, that we go down the slope directly toward the spa rather than backtrack. It wouldn't be easy, but still less taxing than the rugged terrain we'd traverse to get there.

We stuffed the now stiffening body into the sleeping bag and fastened it with the Velcro fasteners. Then, placing the sniper rifle on top of the sleeping bag, we rolled everything into the canvas tent and secured it with the tent ropes. Jason found a ten-foot sapling and, using the knife that I'd removed from the dead man's waist just before we put him in the sleeping bag, cut it down. We hooked the pole through the tent ropes and hefted it to our shoulders. I figured the guy weighed two hundred pounds, but as dead weight, it felt more like two-fifty.

With Jason in the lead, we struck out down the slope toward the spa. Once we were off the ledge, we lost sight of the spa, but Jason seemed to know the way, even though we had to double back a couple of times to make our way around stands of gnarled trees too close together to pass through.

It was nearly four pm when we stumbled out of the trees, just below the manicured lawn to the southwest of the reception building. As we trudged up the slope and walked onto the road, I could see faces peering at us through the windows. Sandra stood in the door, her hands shading her eyes.

After hours of trekking down the hill carrying the body, fighting off the flies and other flying pests that were attracted to the smell of the body, we must have looked a sight. We were drenched in sweat, and clumps of dirt and bits of foliage clung to our clothing and hair. My shoulders felt like someone had stabbed them with hot pokers, and my calves had begun to tighten up again. Out of the rain forest, with its moist smell of sandalwood, fern, flowers, and the excrement of the forest denizens, the smells from the corpse and our sweaty bodies were strong in the air.

We stopped near Jason's ruined jeep and lowered the body. Sandra came running out to me, and, ignoring my rank odor, pulled me close.

"I was getting so worried," she said. She pulled back, wrinkling her nose, and looked at the canvas. "Is that the person who was shooting at us?"

I nodded.

Kono came up behind her. "Who is it?" he asked Jason.

Wiping sweat from his forehead, Jason shook his head. "Damned if I know. Some haole. We'll have to get the body to the state police to see if they can identify him."

"So, no more danger of being shot at?" Kono said, looking at me.

"Not by this guy, at least," I said. But, a tickling sensation in the back of my brain told me there was more to it than this one dead shooter. I kept that thought to myself. "We got anyplace we can store him, and the others? A big freezer, maybe?"

He looked puzzled at me.

"We leave them out like this and pretty soon they'll be stinking the place up something fierce. We need to keep them on ice until the authorities can remove them."

He nodded in understanding. The other two bodies had already been exposed for over a day, and were probably already ripe. He called for a couple of the guys who'd been moving luggage and instructed them to get golf carts and collect the two bodies near the pool. Then, he instructed the goggle-eyed waitresses to clear out the large meat locker in the restaurant kitchen.

After the bodies were safely stored, I went to our cabana and, while Sandra waited, took a long shower. It seemed to take forever to get the grit out of my hair and the folds of skin, and the smell of death still lingered in my nose. I shaved the day's stubble. My skin was tender and sore from prolonged exposure to even the filtered sun I'd been under, stupidly, without a hat, all day. I crumpled the clothes I'd worn and tossed them into the trash can. No way was I ever going to wear them again.

When I'd finally dressed and come out of the shower, Sandra smiled and put her arms around me. "Now, that's more like it," she said, nuzzling my cheek. I winced, but when she started to pull away, I pulled her back. If I've got to be hurt, I'd rather have her do it than anyone I know.

"I guess I must have smelled pretty ripe."

"Rotten is more like it. I've never understood why people say 'ripe' when they describe stinky smells. Things smell good when they're ripe, and you didn't smell good." She laughed and kissed me, a long, deep kiss that took my breath away.

"I guess I smell okay now?"

"And, you taste good, too."

"Speaking of taste, I've only had an MRE to eat all day. I could use some real food."

Charles Ray

22.

_____

When we got to the restaurant, I noticed that Jason had also bathed and changed. He was now wearing jeans and a Hawaiian shirt. He also still wore his gun belt. The badge looked strange pinned to the colorful shirt. He and Kono were sitting at a table by the window, and he had a pile of food in front of him that looked enough to feed a rifle squad. He waved us over when he saw us.

"I don't know about you, Al," he said, as Sandra and I sat down. "But, I'm hungry enough to eat a whole pig."

"Looks like you got most of it in front of you now," I said.

"Shit – sorry, Ma'am," he said to Sandra, with a sheepish look on his face. "This is just the appetizer."

"Why don't you two let me order for you," Kono said. "Before this joker cleans out the kitchen."

Without waiting for our answer, he got up and made a beeline for the kitchen.

The restaurant was almost filled. Quincy and Darren, Sandra had told me, had been moved to their cabanas. Amy was looking after Darren, and Mei Ling hadn't left Quincy's side. The rest of the guests, including Quincy's parents and the Lius, who sat together at a table near the center of the room, were there in twos and fours, except for Marcus Culpepper, who sat across the room from us, alone at a table staring down into a glass that sat in front of him. Everyone had gone quiet when Sandra and I entered, and I noticed heads occasionally turning our way, and little smiles when they caught us looking at them.

"Looks like you two are the men of the hour," Sandra said.

"Yeah," Jason mumbled around a mouthful of food. "They been doing that since I came in. Kinda creepy, you know."

"Get used to it," Sandra said. She laughed as she patted his hand. "When you insist on going out to fight dragons, you have to accept that people are going to look at you as some kind of knight errant."

He looked at me, questions in his eyes.

"Don't fight it, kid," I said. "Unfortunately, she knows what she's talking about."

He shrugged. "I'm just a country cop doing my job, is all. Which reminds me; we need to work out how we're gonna get word down the mountain about this and get the state boys in here to do their stuff."

I glanced out the window. The sky was a pearl gray with pink tints at the fringes of the few wispy clouds I could see, and the shadows were long and stretching across the lush green grass. "How long would it take to walk to the nearest place with a phone?"

"About as long as our trek today took."

"Well, no sense doing it in the dark," I said. "I suppose one of us could do it at first light."

He paused, a fork laden with food halfway to his mouth. He nodded. "Yeah, good point." He smiled. "That means I'm now officially off duty. Darlin', could I have a cold beer?" he said to the waitress who had been standing near. "Guess I should be the one to go, being local law and all. I think you can hold things together until I can get back."

Along with his beer, the waitress brought our food. A large plate of roast pork, mashed potatoes, some kind of green vegetable with bits of pineapple, and chunks of golden brown bread was put in front of me; a plate with human-sized portions of the same thing was put in front of Sandra. "Thank you," I said to the cute young waitress. "Now, could you bring me a large beer as well?" She smiled and scooted off. I turned to Jason. "Yeah, I can handle things."

I took a taste of the pork. It was tender, sweet, with just a hint of tang to the taste. In short, delicious. From the look on Sandra's face, I knew she felt the same.

"You know, Al," Jason said. "You've had this strange expression on your face ever since we got back this afternoon. Something's eating at you; what is it?"

I had to give it to the kid. His cop instincts were pretty good. There *had* been something bothering me. Not just when we came off the mountain either. I think it had been nagging at me from the moment we found the damaged pickup in the storage building.

"Look, we got the shooter," I said. "I'm pretty sure he was up there on that mountain by himself. And, it's entirely possible he was the one who cut the phone lines to cut us off from the outside."

"I agree," he said, nodding. "So, what's bothering you?"

"The pickup. There's no way he could have gotten in here and damaged the pickup without being seen."

His paused, his fork halfway to his mouth. His eyes narrowed in concentration. "Are you saying that someone here was working with this guy?"

"That's what my gut's telling me."

"Then, maybe I shouldn't wait until morning to go for help."

I felt Sandra stiffen next to me. "You two aren't planning to go running around in the dark are you?"

I laid a hand on her arm. "No, babe, we're not." I turned back to Jason. "I don't think that would be a good idea. Better if you wait until morning; that way, whoever it is might not know we suspect anything. If you leave now, it might spook whoever it is. Besides, in the dark it would be easy to ambush you."

He took a deep breath. "I suppose you're right. I wasn't looking forward to doing that anyway."

With it settled that neither Jason nor I would be wandering around in the dark, Sandra's look of worry eased. But, she still regarded me with a skeptical expression. We finished our meal in silence. Jason and I each had another beer, and then Sandra and I left for our cabana as he ordered a third.

We showered and changed into shorts and T-shirts and crawled under the coverlet. I was still a bit fatigued from the day's exertions, so we passed on the sex, content to just lie there cuddling each other. At some point, she fell asleep, her breasts pushing against me as she inhaled. But, she still clung to me as if to ensure I didn't slip out of bed.

23.

The next morning, we rose early, and Sandra and I put on sweats and took a brisk walk around the perimeter of the spa. Afterwards, we did crunches, sit-ups, and pushups in the cabana and, I meditated for ten minutes while Sandra showered. After I'd showered and dressed, we walked down to the restaurant.

It was seven am when we entered the restaurant. Jason was sitting alone by the window with an empty plate in front of him. He was sipping coffee. None of the other guests were there, and there was only one waitress on duty. We joined him.

I ordered pancakes, sausage, hash browns, biscuits and coffee. Sandra ordered scrambled eggs, toast and coffee. The waitress filled our cups with coffee and went off to get the food.

"I'll be taking off as soon as I finish this coffee," he said. "What do you plan to do?"

"I thought I might snoop around and see if I can get some idea who here was helping the shooter."

"Kinda thought you might. You be careful."

"Careful is my middle name."

"Yeah, I saw that yesterday when you - -," Realizing that Sandra was sitting there with her eyes wide, he snapped his mouth shut. Lifting his cup, he glanced apologetically over the rim at me.

"There's no need to do that," Sandra said. "I've known Al long enough to know he probably did something extremely foolhardy out there yesterday."

"Uh, no ma'am, it wasn't like that," Jason mumbled. "I just meant he was about the bravest man I've ever seen. He didn't even have a gun, and he was prepared to face that dude down."

"Hey," I said. "I knew you had my back."

Sandra laid a hand on mine. "Jason, first, stop calling me ma'am. I'm not *that* old." His cheeks flushed a darker tan. "And, secondly, Al's more dangerous without a gun than you can ever imagine."

She would know. She'd seen me go up against more than one armed man and come out whole. She'd never liked it, but she knew what I was capable of.

Jason's eyes narrowed as he looked at me. I think my stock rose a few notches in his estimation. "When I get back up here, you're gonna have to tell me some more about him, ma'am, er, Sandra. He don't talk much about himself."

Before the two of them could talk any more about me, Jason finished his coffee and saluting, left for the long trek down the mountain road. By the time our food arrived, a few of the other guests had begun wandering in.

I watched them as I ate, trying to see if I could get a bead on which of them might be – have been – in cahoots with the dead gun man.

It didn't seem likely it would be someone who didn't have a close connection to Darren Culpepper, and, by now, I was convinced that he had been the original target. In fact, I was coming to the conclusion that he was the only target.

During the wedding rehearsal, there had only been two shots, and as I replayed them in my mind, it seemed clear that he was the intended target for both, missed through sheer luck. He'd moved just before the first shot. Had he not, it would have gone through the center of his back. The .50 caliber round would have probably torn through his heart, or at least nicked a major blood vessel causing him to bleed out before we could help him. The second had missed only because that poor man had chosen that time to stand, putting his head in the path of the bullet. If random killing had been the shooter's aim, when the crowd was panicking and milling around, he had plenty of targets of opportunity, but hadn't taken any. The shots at Jason Kaheamui's jeep were to keep us cut off. From where the gunman was positioned, he could have taken Jason out long before he'd ever reached the spa, yet he hadn't.

So, I decided I'd concentrate my attention on those closest to Darren. Just then, Lane Vandemeer and Shelly Corwin entered the restaurant. They took a table against the window, about two tables away from where Sandra and I sat.

I let them get settled and order their food. "Excuse me, babe," I said to Sandra, picking up my coffee cup. "I need to talk to a few people."

She didn't look up at me, nor did she acknowledge what I said, but I knew she'd heard me. She knew what I was planning. She didn't completely approve, but she understood the need. Or, maybe she had just come to terms that I am what I am.

I walked over to the table. They looked up as I neared. Vandemeer had a noncommittal expression, and looked like he needed a shave. Corwin had dark circles around her bloodshot eyes.

"Hi, folks," I said. "Mind if I join you?"

Corwin nodded and pulled her coffee cup to her lips.

"Sure, pull up a chair," Vandemeer said. "Hey, what you and that cop did yesterday is the talk of the place. Is it true, you found the person who was shooting at us?"

I nodded. "He was using a .50 caliber sniper rifle. Looked military issue."

He leaned forward, his hands clasped around his cup. "Can't say I'm surprised, considering the punch those rounds packed. Any ID on him?"

Jason and I hadn't exactly taken time to pat the corpse down. Not that I'm squeamish about it. Well, maybe I am a little squeamish, but, at the time, our main thought had been to get down off that damn mountain.

"No," I said. "Sergeant Kaheamui's on his way to call for the state police. We're hoping they can identify him."

"Why would anyone want to just shoot at us like that?" Shelly Corwin was looking over the rim of her cup. There was a haunted look in her eyes. "Was this some kind of nut, like that guy in Texas who shot at people from the school bell tower?"

"I don't think so," I said. "I think there was a specific target in this case."

For a moment, he looked stunned. He ran his hand through his hair, growing out now from the military cut he'd worn probably for most of his adult life. I could see his mind working as if his skull was transparent. "You're saying that Darren was the intended target?" He'd come to the same conclusion I had, probably from mentally reviewing the events at the rehearsal. Events that might not be apparent to anyone who'd never been under fire, but in retrospect, obvious to anyone who had. I could see the light of comprehension in his eyes. "But, why; why would anyone want to kill Darren?"

"I was kinda hoping you could help me figure that out. You served with him in the navy. Is there anyone from his past that you know who might have a grudge against him?"

"No, Darren was a respected, well-liked officer . . . no, wait, there's one guy, but, it doesn't make sense."

"Tell me about it."

His eyes screwed up in concentration. "It's

been a while, more than a year in fact. There was this one kid on Darren's team. A tough SEAL, but not all there, if you know what I mean. SEAL team members are trained to be tough, and we're certainly no strangers to violence, but, this kid seemed to like it more than was healthy."

I waited for him to continue. He seemed to be reluctant to go into details, but I knew the details, even the most inconsequential seeming details, could be important. I also knew the bonds of brotherhood that developed among fighting men, especially those in elite units, are tight, making them reluctant to share with outsiders. Finally, he took a deep breath.

"Darren tried working with him. Tried to teach him to distinguish between the needs of combat and appropriate behavior in noncombat situations. But, the kid had the bloodlust. He *enjoyed* killing. The last straw was when they were on a mission down in . . . well, the location's unimportant . . . they're mission was to scout the compound of a drug lord and guide local forces in to take the guy out. He was hiding out there with his family. The kid, Perry Uldrich, was in a position on a hill overlooking the compound with another team member. Their mission was just to observe and report. But, when the target got in a car and looked like he was leaving, Perry decided to stop him. Took him out with a .50 caliber sniper rifle from just over a thousand meters."

"Seems to me he just made an on-the-spot decision," I said. "It happens sometimes."

"Yeah, but the drug lord was in the car with one of his kids, a boy about ten. He was probably just taking the kid to the local village for some shopping. He'd left the rest of the family in the compound."

"Was this Uldrich very experienced in field operations? Maybe he just miscalculated." I didn't believe that. I could almost sense where he was going with his story, but I played devil's advocate to draw him out.

"He'd been on five similar operations. He knew he wasn't supposed to engage the target. But, that wasn't all of it. You know what a .50 caliber round can do? The slug went right through the man and splattered the kid against the inside of the car. Killed them both instantly. And, what did Perry do? He just smiled and said 'two less drug pushers to worry about.' He seemed to actually enjoy it. Well, that was it as far as Darren was concerned. He brought the kid up on charges of insubordination and failure to obey orders. Busted him out of the SEALs, and, if Darren had had his way he would have had him kicked out of the navy on a dishonorable discharge. When the command pushed back on that, he tried for a bad conduct discharge, but they finally compromised and kicked him out on a general discharge. Kid swore he'd make Darren pay for ruining his career."

A dishonorable or bad conduct discharge would not only have ruined a military career, but would have carried over into civilian life. Uldrich would have been forever marked, unable to get a security clearance, and probably would have been passed over for most jobs. The general discharge, used for those who haven't cut it in uniform, was a convenient and relatively hassle-free way to unload yourself of deadwood without making it impossible for them to function as civilians.

"Sounds like he got off easy," I said.

"He did. Besides, the kid went back to Arizona after he got busted out of the navy, and as far as I know, Darren's had no contact with him since. How in hell could he have known Darren would be here? You think he's the shooter?"

I described the corpse we had stored in the restaurant freezer. He agreed that it sounded like Uldrich. I asked him if he'd take a look at it when he finished his breakfast, but he said he'd rather get it over with.

Leaving Corwin picking at her breakfast, we walked through the kitchen to the freezer in the back. The kitchen staff, busy preparing breakfast for the growing crowd of diners, ignored us. I noticed that they also avoided the back of the kitchen nearest the freezer.

I opened the freezer door. The three bodies were laid out, side by side, on the raised plank floor. Ice crystals had formed on the covers that had been draped over them. The sniper's corpse, still wrapped in the sleeping bag, was off to the right, separated from his two victims by three feet. The sniper rifle, now coated with a sheet of ice, lay next to it.

Kneeling down, I gingerly parted the top of the sleeping bag and peeled it aside. In death, with glistening ice crystals coating his hair and eyebrows, the killer looked peaceful. I heard a gasp behind me.

"That's him," Vandemeer said. "That's Perry Uldrich."

24.

When we returned to rejoin Corwin, Vandemeer still looked shaken. As we sat, Corwin looked at him sympathetically and laid a hand on his wrist.

"I can't believe it," he said. "How in hell did he know Darren would be here? It doesn't make sense. It's been a year since he was discharged. He could have gotten at Darren in San Diego anytime. Why here? Why now?"

Those were the very questions I sought answers for. I didn't really think that Vandemeer was involved, but in my line of work, everyone's a suspect until proven otherwise, so I didn't say anything about the possibility of an accomplice still in the spa. First, I wanted to talk to Darren Culpepper.

As I left the two of them, I noticed the look in Corwin's eyes, and the way she massaged his forearm. The dark circles around her eyes were from lack of sleep, but I doubted her lack of sleep had been caused by fear.

Sandra had finished her breakfast and was just about done with her tea when I rejoined her.

"Did you learn anything new?" she asked.

I told her about the shooter. "I need to talk to Culpepper," I said.

"But, now that you and Jason have the man who tried to kill him, isn't it over?"

"It won't be over until I find the person here who was working with the shooter."

Her eyes were like two small demitasse saucers. "You mean there's still a possible killer around?"

"Yeah, afraid so, and if I can't identify and stop him – or her – Culpepper could still be in danger."

She put her cup down and stood. She knew what I had to do, and, whether or not she liked it, she knew I would do it. One of the reasons I think I love her like I do is that way she has of going with the flow when it comes to my approach to life. We don't say it to each other often – I have trouble remembering the last time either of us seriously said 'I love you' to the other, but, we both *know* it, and know that when it counts, we'll be there for each other.

She took my hand as we left the restaurant and started down the path toward the cabana that Darren Culpepper was now sharing with his bride-to-be.

I knocked on the door. "Come in, it's not locked," Amy Liu's voice said from inside.

"You should consider keeping it locked," I said as we entered.

She was sitting on the side of the bed, spooning soup into his mouth. He lay there, the coverlet at his waist, propped against the pillows. Some of the color was coming back into his face, but there were dark circles under his eyes. He was bare from the waist up except for the makeshift bandage, torn sheets, wrapped around his right shoulder. A slight red smudge near the center, some blood seepage, marked where the bullet had exited. He winced in pain as he turned to look at us.

"How are you feeling?" I asked as I approached the side of the bed.

"Like I was in a pissing contest with a water buffalo, and the buffalo won," he said with a wan smile.

The skin around the edge of the bandage was a mixture of red and blue. He would need professional medical attention soon, I thought. There was danger that the wound would become infected. I reached over and felt his forehead. He was warm to the touch, just a touch of fever. That could be the sign of the beginning of an infection, or just a reaction to the injury. I turned my attention to Amy Liu.

"I still think you should keep the door locked, just for extra safety," I said.

"My parents dropped by earlier and said you and Jason had caught the person who was shooting at us, so we should be okay now, right?"

There are two ways to deal with bad news: soft pedal it; talk around it until people get the message; or, just hit them between the eyes with it. I can be diplomatic, and for Amy's sake probably should have, but I didn't think Darren Culpepper was the type who did a lot of beating around the bush.

"We got the shooter, yeah," I said. "But, I think someone among the people here was working with him, and that means there's still a chance they might come after Darren again."

Her light brown complexion went ashen and her eyes widened. Darren looked up at me with a level gaze. He didn't seem surprised at what I'd said.

"So, I was the shooter's intended target?" He

asked it the way he would have asked me the time. No surprise. No shock.

I nodded.

"When the pain eased enough for me to think clearly, I sort of came to that conclusion. Who was the shooter?"

I told him. "But, I don't think he was working alone."

Now, it was his turn to nod. "You're more than likely right. Uldrich hated my guts for getting him kicked out of the navy, but he had plenty time to come after me before I left San Diego, and didn't. Besides, there's no way he'd know I was here unless someone told him."

"My thoughts exactly. Now, the question is; who here is pissed enough at you to do that?"

"Other than Amy and her family, my brother Marcus, Lane and Shelly, I don't really know the other people here," he said. "There are one or two cousins or uncles or something, I haven't seen them in a long time. Actually, Marcus took care of invitations for those on our side, about eight in all. The others are Amy's friends or relatives."

"You and Vandemeer get along okay?"

A brief look of anger flared in his eyes. "Lane's my best friend. We went through SEAL training together, and have been assigned at the same base for a long time. I'd trust him with my life. There's no way he'd be involved in anything that would hurt me. Hell, I'm making him the chief operating officer of my . . . family's company."

"What about Ms. Corwin? How well do you know her?"

"Shelly's good people," he said, still glaring angrily at me. "I got to know her in San Diego. She loves the environment and offered to work with the navy to help us operate in ways that minimized negative impacts. I find I agree with her views, which is why I asked her to join the company as an environmental specialist. Besides, in case you haven't noticed, she and Lane are a little sweet on each other."

"I had noticed, in fact. And, for the record, I agree with you; I don't think either of them is involved. But, I wanted to get them out of the way. Now, let's think about who here wants you dead."

"Heck, I can think of one or two people on my company's board who wouldn't shed any tears at my funeral, but they're not here, and I can't really see them hiring a hit man. Most of the people here, like I said, I have no connection with. I can't think of anyone here who fits that profile."

I noticed that Amy Liu, who had been sitting quietly, gently massaging his uninjured shoulder as we talked, was leaning forward, her body tense.

"Amy," I said. "Do you have something you want to say?"

"Well, I'm not sure if I should. I mean, Darren's right; most of the people here don't know him that well, and those that do like him. It's difficult to believe that anyone would want to hurt him."

The tension in her voice, and body language, though, belied her words. "I sense that you're thinking there might be an exception to that."

She looked pleadingly at Darren. He lifted his good hand and laid it on her thigh. "Go ahead, sweetheart," he said. "Say what's on your mind."

"Well, it's just . . . I mean . . . oh, Darren, darling, you know I love him, but you have to admit, he has been angry a lot lately."

He closed his eyes. His chest lifted in a sigh. "No, that's not possible. I know he can be headstrong and impulsive, but I can't believe he'd actually want to hurt me."

"Who are we talking about, folks?" I asked.

He looked up at me. There was sadness in his eyes. "My brother, Marcus," he said. "We had some words earlier in the week, and he's been upset ever since I came back home."

Charles Ray

25.

I hadn't paid much attention to the younger Culpepper. As is often the fate of younger brothers, Marcus Culpepper been more or less in the background. Not just during the run-up to Darren's wedding, but for his entire life.

It took some coaxing, but bit by bit, the saga of the Culpepper siblings came out.

Older by four years, the weight of responsibility had fallen upon Darren's shoulders when his brother, Marcus, was born. His mother had died shortly after giving birth, and Marcus had been raised by a succession of nannies and tutors, his father, Henry Culpepper, too busy making a success of the construction company he'd inherited from his own father.

As the two brothers grew, Darren had become more mature and responsible, while Marcus, as often happens with the baby of a family, grew into an impetuous, self-centered individual, more concerned with fast cars and faster women than studies or learning the business. When Darren graduated from high school in Kahului and gone off to the mainland, spending four years at Stanford University, Marcus was just starting high school. Without his stable older brother around to bail him out of trouble, or knock sense into his head when he was tempted to go astray, he'd had a rough four years, barely graduating in his senior year, and then only because his father had donated money to build a football stadium for the school.

After high school, Marcus had started working in his father's company, doing odd office jobs, and occasionally going out on construction projects where the foremen tolerated him because he was the boss's son, never carrying his share of the load and in general making a nuisance of himself. His father finally realized that he'd never work out in the field, gave him the title Director of Public Relations, complete with a private office and a secretary, and ignored him.

Darren, in the meantime, had graduated from Stanford and, having done Naval ROTC, accepted a commission in the navy for a chance to see the world and get his bearings. He'd easily qualified for the elite SEALs and in a few short years had been promoted to lieutenant commander and given command of a team.

In the navy, Darren Culpepper discovered the life he really wanted to lead, and was seriously considering making it a career. But, in his tenth year of service, he'd received an urgent telegram from his father's attorney. His father had been diagnosed with terminal lung cancer and given just six months to live. The old man wanted Darren to leave the navy and take the helm of the family business.

Ever the responsible son, Darren didn't even consider ignoring his father's request. Twenty-four hours after receiving the telegram, he'd submitted his resignation papers, said goodbye to his team, and boarded a flight from San Diego to Honolulu.

Back home, he'd tried to convince his dying father to turn the business over to Marcus, but the old man was insistent. While he loved his youngest son, he knew, having watched his dissolute life style for a decade, that Marcus had neither the intelligence nor the will to take over the business, and would, in fact, destroy it through neglect.

The turn of events hadn't pleased young Marcus. He'd assumed that he, the son who stayed home, would naturally be the heir to the throne. Just hours before he breathed his last, though, Henry Culpepper had dashed such hopes by calling the two to his side and announcing that Darren would take over the company. Marcus would retain his title, office, and salary, but would have no say in the operation of the business.

"He wasn't happy about it," Darren said. "Not happy at all. But, you never argued with my father. In truth, though, I don't think Marcus really wanted the responsibility, it was just the thought of being in charge that attracted him. I think he's come to terms with it now."

"But, you know he's siding with those on the board who oppose the changes you want to make," Amy said.

"He'll get over it. They all will. The changes *will* be made, and when they see that they will make us a better company, they'll all come around."

"But, still," I said. "Your brother does have a reason to be upset with you."

"Sure, but what brothers don't have issues? He's impetuous, but not violent. The only person Marcus has ever really hurt is himself."

"You're forgetting what he did when you first wanted Lane to be your best man," Amy said.

I gave him a querying look. He sighed. "Well, yeah, he did pitch a hissy fit about that. That was my fault, though. I should have known better. It's just that Lane and I've been friends for so long, he was the first person I thought of. Marcus insisted, though, that as my brother, he should be the best man. Lane understood, and offered to step aside. Marcus calmed down after that. Look, Al, if you're trying to say you think my brother is somehow involved in an effort to hurt me, I just refuse to believe it. My brother is self-indulgent, but he's not violent."

I imagine Abel would have said the same thing before Cain, in a fit of jealous rage, bashed his head in.

Charles Ray

26.

I wasn't going to convince Darren Culpepper that his brother was in on an attempt to kill him. Fact is, I didn't have any evidence that pointed at him, other than that nagging, itchy feeling you get at the back of your neck when you know something, but you don't know exactly what it is you know, or how you know it.

I left them there, after getting Amy to promise to keep the door locked, and escorted Sandra to our cabana. I gave her a peck on the cheek and told her I had a private errand to run. The look she gave me told me she knew where I was going.

I wandered back up to the bar, meaning to ask Kono the number of Marcus Culpepper's cabana, but I found the younger man sitting at the end of the bar. It wasn't even nine am and he was already nursing a Bloody Mary. His bloodshot eyes indicated that it wasn't his first.

"Hey," he said, as I sat on the stool next to him. "The big hero. Hear you and that cop got the guy who shot up the place. Lemme buy you a drink." His voice was slurred, and his head bobbed up and down as he spoke. I decided that this wasn't even his *second* drink.

"No thanks; it's a bit early for me." I asked the bartender for a cup of coffee.

He took a long drink, allowing some of the liquor to spill over his chin. "Never too late for a drink," he said. "Never too late for a drink."

His bloodshot eyes regarded me warily over the rim of his glass.

"Do you know anyone here who'd want to hurt your brother?" I asked.

He blinked. Then, he put his glass down. "My brother? Who would want to hurt my brother?" His head bobbed up and down. "Everybody loves Darren . . . they always have . . . Darren, the good one. Nobody would want to hurt Darren."

I looked in to his eyes. Red lines crisscrossed his pupils, which had a reddish tint at the bottom. He looked at me with a haunted look, a mixture of sadness and – something else that I could not fathom – a longing to unburden himself to someone. At times like this, with people like Marcus Culpepper, it's often best to simply serve as a willing ear and let them talk. The bartender brought my coffee, which he slid across the bar in front of me. I picked up the cup and sipped slowly, gazing at Culpepper.

"You know," he said. "Darren was always the lucky one, always the one people turned to." He was playing with his drink now, turning the glass around in slightly overlapping circles, making little curved marks on the bar's surface. "You'd think the baby of the family would be the one who got all the good treatment. Not in the Culpepper family, oh no, not the most serious Culpeppers. Dad always turned to Darren." He wiped at a tear that had formed in his left eye. "I think he blamed me for mother's death, you see. She died right after I was born."

He then just sat there, tapping his finger on the rim of his glass, looking at me. He wanted me to say something; but, what? So, he'd had it rough – at least, according to the way he looked at things. But, who hadn't had it rough? Still, though, I wanted to keep him talking; I knew he had something else on his mind, but he needed encouragement to walk into that seldom-visited space, that room, behind whose door lay the thing he wanted to bring out into the open.

"Must have been tough on you," I said. "Growing up with something like that hanging over your head."

His laugh was harsh and guttural. "Tough? Man, you don't know fucking tough. I mean, my old man blamed me for my mother's death – like if I hadn't been born or something, maybe she wouldn't have died, and it would just be the three of them. Yeah, it was tough having to live in the shadow of a perfect person, a person you could never hope to live up to."

He took another long, desperate swallow of the Bloody Mary, draining the glass. Putting the glass on the bar, he shoved it away, knocking it over, and ordered another.

"Hey, buggah, hana hou, and make it a double this time," he said. "Not watered down like the last one." The bartender looked at me, shrugging and raising his eyebrows. I nodded. "Darren was the prince," he continued as the bartender mixed his drink. "Star of the football team, homecoming king, straight A's in all his classes. He could do no wrong. Hell, if he fell into a pile of shit, he'd come up with a fistful of diamonds." The bartender put the new drink in front of him. "Put it on my tab, bra." He lifted the drink and took a long pull, smacking his lips in satisfaction. "I went out for football; my junior year; but, when the coach found a couple of joints in my locker, he kicked me off the team. Only reason they didn't expel me from the damn school is my old man built 'em a new football stadium. I wasn't akamai like Darren either. Never got good grades, just good enough to be passed."

"You ever think you're a bit hard on yourself? I mean, you seem to be trying to make people dislike you, like calling the bartender bugger. That's not nice."

"Naw, bra, I called him buggah, that's Hawaiian for chap or fellow. Now, that's one thing I can do better than Darren. I did learn the local lingo from the mokes I hung with. They were some big, bad dudes, but with my allowance money, they didn't seem to mind a skinny haole being part of their gang. Darren got along with the locals well enough, but he never hung with the wild ones like I did."

Another drink. He wiped his lips with the back of his hand.

"Anyway, when he left for college, I thought I'd finally be out from under his shadow, that people would quit judging me by his actions. It took a while, but when he graduated and joined the navy, and the old man took me into the company, I thought it was over, you know. I mean, he gave me a title and an office; even let me have my own private secretary. I was sure he was planning for me to eventually take over the business. But, no, not after I stayed here at his beck and call all these years. When the doctors told him he was about to get his ticket punched, the old bastard called Darren back to take over."

"That's natural, isn't it; the elder brother

taking over from the father?"

"Fuck natural!" Little specks of spittle flew from his mouth, and a thin red line of Bloody Mary dribbled from the corner of his mouth. "I earned the right. It wasn't Darren who stayed by the old man's side all those years, putting up with the smell of death that was there long before he finally died, putting up with his demands and criticisms. No, it was me, and I deserved to take over, not Darren. There ain't nothing natural or fair about it. If that fucking dipshit Uldrich had been a better shot, things would be the way they're supposed to be."

I stared at him. Despite the amount of alcohol he'd consumed, he knew he'd said too much. Other than Jason and me, Lane Vandemeer was the only other person at the spa who knew the shooter's identity – other than his accomplice. His mouth snapped shut, and his eyes darted from side to side. His hand, resting against the side of the glass, shook enough to cause a ripple in the drink.

27.

As soon as I confronted him, the words gushed forth. Alternately crying and cursing, Marcus Culpepper confessed to hiring the ex-SEAL Perry Uldrich to kill his brother.

He and I were still sitting at the bar, having skipped lunch, he with his head resting on his arm, barely conscious after downing three more doubles, me nursing my second cup of coffee, which had gone cold, when the *babbety-de-babbety* of an approaching helicopter rattled the large windows of the restaurant.

A bird landed, and shortly afterwards took off to be replaced by another. Pretty soon, Jason came into the restaurant, followed by what looked like every cop assigned to the island of Maui, a few in plain clothes, and some in tactical gear, complete with helmets, flak jackets, and riot weapons. The place buzzed with excitement as the group entered.

Spotting me, he came over with a square jawed six footer in tow, who he introduced as Lieutenant Vincent Gilhoolie, of the Hawaii State Police, and senior man on Maui. I introduced Marcus Culpepper and gave Gilhoolie a summary of what he'd just finished telling me. Marcus mumbled something and nodded his head when Gilhoolie asked him if what I said was true. Gilhoolie had one of the other plain clothes detectives handcuff him and take him outside to the last helicopter, which sat on the helipad with its rotors swinging slowly. "Take him down to Kahului and put him in a holding cell until we get things sorted here," he said.

"There are three corpses in the freezer," I said. "One is the shooter."

"Yeah, Sergeant Kaheamui told me," Gilhoolie said gruffly. "Meat wagon from the ME's office should be here soon, along with busses to take everyone down to Kahului. Afraid the spa's now a crime scene, and after we question the guests, we'll have to vacate the premises."

Kono walked in at that point. "Do you really have to shut us down?" he asked plaintively. "Business will be bad enough when word gets out people were killed here."

Gilhoolie's glare left no doubt in anyone's mind what he thought about Xanadu's financial situation. According to *his* book of rules, you secured the crime scene, and, by damn, he would *secure* the crime scene. Kono looked like a whipped puppy as he turned and, with shoulders slumped, left the bar.

Gilhoolie snorted. "Jackson," he yelled at a tall uniformed officer. "They get up the mountain to retrieve that pilot's body yet?"

The officer ducked his head and put a hand to his ear. After mumbling something and nodding, he looked up. "Yeah, lieutenant," he said. "The body's on the way back to town and they're sending a pilot up to retrieve the helicopter as soon as our techs finish examining it. They found the campsite Sergeant Kaheamui mentioned, too, and that's been secured."

Gilhoolie nodded. His expression was as close to a smile as I'd seen since he walked in. I had a feeling this was as happy as he ever got. He turned his attention to me.

"The sergeant already told me what you two did up on the mountain," he said. "But, I'd still like your version, as well as what happened before he arrived on the scene."

I took him through everything from the

moment I stepped off the helicopter from Oahu up until Marcus Culpepper confessed to hiring someone to kill his brother. It has only been a few days, but it felt like an eternity. "I get the sense this was a last minute plan," I said. "During one of their conversations, Darren mentioned the disgruntled seaman he'd gotten cashiered from the navy, and Marcus saw his opportunity."

"Guy must have been a real fuckup to miss like he did," Gilhoolie said.

"A fuckup he might have been, but it was just dumb luck that he missed. That first shot would have killed Culpepper if he hadn't moved when he did. Same with the second shot; if that old guy hadn't stood, it would have hit him. No, Uldrich was an expert sniper; hell, he made those two shots from almost two thousand yards."

"The guy was kicked out of the navy," Gilhoolie said. "How in hell did he come by a sniper rifle?"

"I don't know how it is here in Hawaii, lieutenant, but, back on the mainland, it's too damn easy to get weapons – even something like a sniper rifle. Hell, in some places you can order them on the Internet. Tobacco's regulated tighter than guns in some states."

He made that snorting sound again. "Keep 'em from getting killed by second hand smoke, so they can be offed in a drive by. Makes a perverted kind of sense, I suppose."

28.

While the bulk of the guests were taken to the Kahului airport and flown to Honolulu by one of the charter services, Gordon Liu rented a big 12-passenger helicopter to take his family, Darren, Quincy and his parents, Mei Ling Chao, Sandra and me to Oahu. He'd called ahead, and ambulances were awaiting us at the Honolulu airport to transport Darren and Quincy to a hospital near Waikiki. Amy road with Darren, and Mei Ling sat next to the stretcher carrying Quincy. He didn't seem to mind her attentions at all.

Sandra and I took a cab from the airport to a small inn three blocks up from the beach, on Kapiolani Boulevard. It was a typical tourist motel, three three-story buildings forming three sides of a square, with a ten-foot-high wrought iron fence on the street side forming the fourth side. The buildings were white stucco with red slate roofs. Palm trees dotted the area inside the square, in the center of which was a kidney-shaped swimming pool with a palm-frond-roofed bar beside it. We got a room on the third floor on the back side of the compound, which actually was the side that faced Waikiki, and from our window we could see the ritzy hotels that lined the beach.

After unpacking our suitcases, we walked down toward Ala Wai, in the direction of the beach, stopping to eat noodles at a food stand on Kuhio. After we finished the noodles, washed down with cold beer, we walked along Waikiki Beach, as far as Fort DeRussey, listening to the crashing of the surf and looking at the glow of the whitecaps as they were stirred by the wind. We walked hand in hand, silently drinking in the dark beauty, and, after reaching the section of beach used by vacationing GIs who were staying at the big military-run hotel near Fort DeRussey, we cut through the shrub and vine lined paths toward Ala Moana Boulevard, and then cut north back to our motel.

The hum of traffic on Kapiolani, and the occasional dull thrum of a jet making departing the airport and straining to gain altitude before banking either right or left, depending upon whether its destination was the mainland or some point west was in sharp contrast to the sounds of bird calls we'd been listening to for five days – kind of comforting in a way, a sure sign that we were back in civilization.

We were up on Friday at dawn, as the sun was just beginning to glint off the hotels and office towers of Waikiki. Traffic on Kapiolani was light, so we jogged along the sidewalk, west toward Chinatown, and then back, where we did a few quick laps in the pool. Back in the room, I meditated while Sandra showered and dressed. Then, I scrubbed the sweat away and dressed, and we went across and down Kapiolani to a pancake restaurant that specialized in early breakfast.

After breakfast, we went outside and hailed a cab to take us to the hospital.

Our first stop was Quincy's room, a private room on the third floor of the gleaming white structure located in the north part of town. The interior walls were a tasteful, pastel beige finish that looked like polished velvet fabric, the floors were a salmon-colored tile, and soft music flowed from hidden speakers. Doctors, nurses, and other medical personnel, went quietly but briskly about their business. Not at all like the hospitals I'd been in before – but, this was obviously a place of healing for those who had the means to pay for ambience.

A nurse was just leaving as we arrived. Mei Ling Chao sat on a chair at the head of the bed, spooning a grayish concoction in to Quincy's mouth. She beamed a broad smile at us. Quincy grimaced.

"Hey, pal," I said. "You look like you're still in pain. I thought the doctor said you just had a minor wound."

"The wound doesn't hurt," he said. "But, this swill they keep making me eat hurts like the dickens."

"Oh, stop being such a baby and eat your oatmeal," Mei Ling said, holding the spoon in front of his mouth as if she was feeding an infant.

Actually, the way he kept twisting his head to the side and making faces, he did look like an oversized baby refusing to eat its carrots.

"I'd rather have bacon and eggs," he said.

"The doctor said you lost blood and your system's weak," she said, holding his head with one hand while she forced the spoon between his lips. "You need to eat soft food for a couple days until your system strengthens."

"Hmphf, ngish," he said. He swallowed. "I'm never gonna get my strength back eating this stuff."

Sandra walked over and sat on the side of the bed opposite Mei Ling.

"Men are such babies," she said. "You want

me to hold him down while you feed him?"

"Yes, unless he starts cooperating."

He looked at me, panic in his eyes.

"Sorry, pal," I said. "I'm not getting in the middle of this. Seems to me, it would be less painful to go ahead and eat the stuff."

"Damn, you're all in it with the doctors, aren't you? Hell, okay." He docilely allowed Mei Ling to finish spooning the lumpy oatmeal in, grimacing as he chewed and swallowed. She fussed over him like a baby, and I noticed a sly gleam in his eyes. Damn if he wasn't enjoying himself.

We informed him that Gordon Liu had called and said they'd decided to stop tempting fate and would have a local priest come to the hospital and perform Amy and Darren's marriage rites in his room just after noon. Along with the immediate family, the four of us were invited.

Mei Ling was daubing at Quincy's chin as we left, and over her head, when Sandra wasn't looking, he winked.

We asked directions to Darren's room at the reception desk in the large entrance lobby. He'd been placed in a larger private room on the second floor, a room large enough to hold two rooms the size of the one Quincy was in, and I'd thought that was far too big for a single patient.

Darren was on the bed, propped up in a sitting position. Amy sat at his side, holding his left hand. Gordon Liu and his wife stood on the other side, with Constance at their side. Lane Vandemeer and Shelly Corwin stood at the foot of the bed. Sandra and I joined them. His coloring had improved, and, now that his wound had been properly dressed, and his right arm put in a sling that kept the arm tight against his body, he didn't seem to be in any pain.

"Welcome, guys," he said as we approached. "Glad you could make it."

"Papa says the priest should be here any minute," Amy said.

"It's not exactly the wedding I'd planned for you two," Gordon Liu said. "But, I don't think we should tempt fate." He smiled wanly.

His wife frowned up at him. "You planned? I did all the work. But, I guess it better to do it this way."

Darren looked up at me and smiled. "Don't worry, Mama Liu," he said. "We really appreciate what you did. Right now, though, all I want to do is marry your daughter. We don't need a fancy ceremony; just our family and close friends is enough. I'm just sorry you had to spend all that money and go to such effort. I do have one thing to ask, though; I need to speak to Al privately."

Mrs. Liu made a gurgling sound in the back of her throat, but her husband put a hand on her arm. With slightly puzzled looks, everyone filed out of the room. At the door, Gordon Liu paused and looked back. "We'll let you know when the priest arrives."

"This won't take long," he said. When the door closed, he waved me closer. "Al, I just wanted to thank you personally. Your quick thinking probably prevented a catastrophe."

"I didn't really do anything," I said. "It all happened too fast."

I had the feeling he wanted to say more. He seemed to be wrestling with whatever it was. Finally, he heaved a deep sigh. "Look, things are a mess. I imagine, because two people were killed, my brother will be charged as an accessory to murder. But, I just wanted you to understand; he's really not a bad person. He's just confused. He's always been the baby, and unfortunately, I wasn't around to help him during the past ten years. If I hadn't stayed away so long, things might have been different."

"Look, I think I know what you're going through right now. When my wife and son were killed in an auto accident, I blamed myself for a long time. If I'd been there with them, it wouldn't have happened – and, I know that's a lie. Hell, if I'd been with them, we all would have probably died anyway. I don't know your brother, but I do know that you're not doing him any good by taking the blame for his decisions and actions. He made his choices, and now, he has to live with them. As for you; you have your own life to worry about. The only way you'll keep from going crazy is to do your best to make *your* life the best you can."

It was harsh, and he probably resented my bluntness. But, it had to be said. If he resented what I said, though, he didn't show it, and in that moment I knew he'd be okay. He'd come from the same environment as his brother, but, because people expected him to be the responsible one, he'd developed into just that. Marcus had lived down to what had been expected of him. He'd had a choice of the road to take, and had taken the wrong one. I doubt there was anything Darren could have done to change that. Deep down, I think he knew that too.

"Well, I'll still do what I can to help him. Anyway, I just wanted you to know how much I appreciate you putting yourself out the way you did. And, if there's ever anything I can do for you, you know where I'll be."

I shook his left hand. I had a feeling he'd be okay.

When I looked outside, the priest had arrived, and everyone was looking expectantly at the door.

I opened the door to let them enter. The priest, a young Hawaiian who looked uncomfortable in his dark jacket and stiff white collar, stood at the head of the bed, beside Amy who clutched Darren's left hand. Vandemeer and Corwin stood on the other side, along with Constance. Liu and his wife stood with Sandra and me at the foot of the bed.

It wasn't a fancy ceremony; no music, no flowers, just a brief, simple exchange of vows, but by the time the priest said "I now pronounce you husband and wife," all the women were crying.

30.

After the wedding, Sandra and I went back to our motel, and spent the rest of the day exploring each other's bodies in the air conditioned comfort of our room. That evening, as the shadows of dusk stretched across the streets, and the lights of Waikiki twinkled, we walked to a hotel on the beach that was offering a luau and stuffed ourselves with roast pig, poi, pineapple, and assorted other delicacies, washed down with Singapore Slings served with little umbrellas carved from pineapple slices, which we also ate.

After eating, we walked along the beach until it was too dark to see the waves curling in over the sand. Back in our room, just before the stroke of midnight, we dumped our clothes in an untidy pile at the foot of the bed and resumed our explorations, finally falling asleep as the sky outside was beginning to turn pale gray signaling the approach of dawn.

We slept in most of Saturday, rousing finally around noon and went out for lunch which consisted of bowls of steaming ramen noodles with iced coffee laced with sweetened condensed milk. Then, we went back to the beach and spent the rest of the afternoon, lounging on mats we rented from a young girl who had a kiosk at the corner of one of the hotels on the beach, lying on our backs beneath a large orange and white umbrella, watching sea gulls dive bomb the area behind the combers that raked the beach, and fighting each other over the scraps thrown on the sand by tourists who'd ignored the signs warning them not to do this.

As the sun sank low in the west, and a breeze picked up, creating little white froth along the tops of the waves that rolled onto the beach, we returned the mats and umbrella and headed back to our motel, stopping for noodles again on the way.

Once we were back in our room, we packed our things, leaving out the clothes we planned to wear on our return flight to Washington, and our suitcases, packed with everything but our toiletries and sleep togs, opened on the floor at the foot of the bed.

Even though our flight wasn't until eight pm

the next evening, we'd decided to check out of the motel early and spend the day touring the city, and then going to the airport early to wait. Both of us were anxious to get back to the familiar territory of DC. Hawaii is nice, but one can only spend so much time on the beach watching the waves and sea gulls.

Maybe it was the briskness of the sea air, or maybe it was just that it was the first time in a long time we'd had time just to be together, but, our lovemaking that night was longer and gentler than it had been in a long time. Afterwards, before we finally drifted off to sleep, we lay there, side by side, our shoulders touching, not talking; just letting our mutual warmth enfold us.

The next morning, just as we were about to leave the room, the phone rang. Sandra, who was closer, picked it up and after saying hello, listened for a few seconds, and then proffered the handset toward me. "It's for you," she said.

"Yes," I said into the phone.

"Al, Jason Kaheamui here. Man, I been trying to find you since last night. I finally had to call Mr. Liu to find out where you were staying."

"Jason, nice hearing your voice. Hope everything's working out okay."

"Yeah, everything's copasetic. Look, I just

wanted to say goodbye before you took off for the mainland, and to thank you for all you did."

"My pleasure, amigo, but I couldn't have done it without you."

"Hey, it was a pleasure working with you, bra; like being back in the rangers. I also wanted to update you on how things shook out." He said that Marcus Culpepper had fully confessed to his role in the attempt to kill his brother. When Darren, shortly after returning home, and during a chat with his brother and his dying father, was talking about his life in the navy and had mentioned the situation he'd had with the ex-SEAL Perry Uldrich, the idea of using the disgruntled man to solve his on problem had been hatched. He'd queried Darren about the incident and learned that Uldrich lived in Arizona. With the help of a detective agency, he'd located the man and made his offer, in addition to getting his revenge against Darren for getting him kicked out of the navy, he'd get ten thousand dollars, five of which had been wired to him to seal the deal. The state police had discovered that the sniper rifle Uldrich used had been part of a shipment of weapons destined for one of the military units in Hawaii that had been hijacked from the port in Oahu. Uldrich had used some of his old service contacts to acquire it, and the police throughout Hawaii were working overtime to try and identify them and locate the remainder of the hijacked shipment. He laughed as he mentioned that last item, saying that they were probably on a private boat on the way to the mainland, or even more likely, on the way to one of the drug armies in Southeast Asia.

"Anyway," Jason continued. "Darren and old man Liu called the state's attorney, pleading for him to cut a deal and go easy on Marcus. He'll do time, but they won't prosecute him for murder, which they could. Hell, he'll probably be out in five or ten years."

Money and influence, even here in this Pacific paradise, always has the last word. "That's the way the world works, my friend," I said. "That's why guys like you will always have a job."

"And, it's why we'll always need guys like you around," he said. "Have a safe trip, bra. Let me know if you're back this way anytime. Maybe next time we can see the rain forest without having to worry about some moke drilling holes in us."

He was laughing when I broke the connection.

I hadn't responded to his invitation. I'd had enough of paradise. Like the Garden of Eden, it had too many snakes.

Sandra and I checked out and called a cab to take us to the airport. It took some doing, but we talked a friendly woman at the United

Airlines check-in counter into allowing us to check our bags way early, and then went back outside and hailed a cab to take us to the Battleship Memorial. We arrived, and, luckily, were able to get two tickets for the last program for the U.S.S. Arizona Memorial, which began at three pm.

The visit to U.S.S. Arizona seemed a fitting end to our trip. The 184-foot-long gleaming white structure, which spans the central section of the battleship, sunk when Japanese warplanes attacked Pearl Harbor on December 7, 1941, is the final resting place for many of the ship's 1,177 crewmen who were killed during that attack. Accustomed to the chatter of groups touring the monuments in DC, the solemn quietness of those touring the memorial's three sections; the entry room, the assembly room where ceremonies are often held, and the shrine room where the names of those killed on the Arizona are engraved on the marble walls; was unnerving and impressive at the same time. Some gazed in awe at the row upon row of names while others stood before the stark white wall with heads bowed. In a quiet voice, our guide pointed out that the mighty vessel had been struck by a bomb that hit the forward magazine, causing a huge explosion that sank one of the largest navy ships of its time in nine minutes.

After the tour we decided to return to the airport and wait in the airline lounge until our flight. Neither of us felt like talking.

Boarding for our flight began at half past seven. We'd managed to get seats in the rear of the economy class cabin, in the center row of three seats, and the right aisle seat was empty. It was a Sunday night flight, and coming so close to July 4, was only half full. We settled in, and Sandra decided to sit in the center seat, her hand resting lightly on my wrist.

We'd been further lucky in that this would be a nine-hour nonstop flight all the way to Dulles Airport. No changing planes on the West Coast.

The sky, or what we could see of it from where we sat, was inky black when we finally lifted off the runway, with the blinking lights of Honolulu briefly glimpsed as we banked left to head for the mainland. The cabin lights were dimmed. There was just the spotty glow of individual reading lights in front of us as a few passengers decided to read, waiting for the meal service that would come at about the halfway point across the Pacific.

I didn't expect to sleep. I can never sleep on a plane in flight; never could; no matter how long the flight. I fall asleep if it's a long flight, but the slightest change in altitude or orientation, or the slightest noise – and, there's always noise, a ping here or a hiss there – and I'm awake, making me more tired than just staying awake. Sometimes I read. If the inflight movie is something I haven't seen before, I watch it. Otherwise, I just sit and stare up at the overhead compartments. It was easier when I was in the army. Then, I'd more often than not been strapped into a parachute and knew that my journey would end before the plane landed.

I put the seat back to allow some leg room, and rested my head against the lumpy pillow they put on each seat. Next to me, Sandra did the same. The pressure of her hand on my wrist increased. I turned to see her smiling at me.

"It's good to be going home," she whispered.

"Yeah, it is that," I said.

She leaned in against me, her head resting on my shoulder. Her silky hair felt good against my cheek, and the warmth of her shoulder was comforting.

Twenty minutes into the flight, the even rise and fall of her breasts indicated that she was fast asleep.

Other books by this author

Buffalo Soldier history series
Buffalo Soldier: Trial by Fire
Buffalo Soldier: Homecoming
Buffalo Soldier: Incident at Cactus Junction
Buffalo Soldier: Peacekeepers

Al Pennyback mysteries
Color Me Dead
Memorial to the Dead
Deadline
Dead, White, and Blue
A Good Day to Die
The Day the Music Died
Die, Sinner
Deadly Intentions
Death by Design
Till Death Do Us Part
Deadly Dose
Dead Man's Cove
Dead Men Don't Answer
Death From Unnatural Causes

Other fiction
Angel on His Shoulder
She's No Angel
Child of the Flame
Pip's Revenge
Wallace in Underland
Further Adventures of Wallace in Underland: Wallace Saves the King
Dead Letters and Other Tales (a collection of short stories)*
The White Dragons: A novel of international intrigue

Nonfiction
Things I Learned from My Grandmother About Leadership and Life
Taking Charge: Effective Leadership for the Twenty-first Century
Grab the Brass Ring
African Places: A Photographic Journey Through Zimbabwe and southern Africa

*Available only as an e-Book for Nook at Barnes and Noble.com. Other books available at most retail book sites in paperback or on Amazon.com for Kindle.

ABOUT THE AUTHOR

Charles Ray has been writing fiction since his teens, winning a Sunday school magazine short story contest for his first publication. His first full-length work was a book on leadership, but with *Die Sinner*, the first in his Al Pennyback mystery series, he returned to his first love, fiction. He has worked as a journalist for newspapers and magazines in Asia and the U.S., and wrote essays, poetry, and editorials for media in Africa and Europe as well. In addition to writing, he is an accomplished photographer and artist. He was editorial cartoonist for the Spring Lake (NC) News during the 1970s and regularly published cartoons in a number of publications such as Ebony, Eagle and Swan, and Essence. A frequent contributor to Yahoo!, he also writes for a number of other online news sites.

He served in the U.S. Army for 20 years, retiring in 1982 and joining the U.S. Foreign Service, where he served for 30 years before retiring in 2012. He's worked and traveled throughout the world. A native of Texas, he now calls Maryland home, when he's not globetrotting looking for new mountains to climb or new adventures to document. Visit his web site at http://charlesaray.blogspot.com, his blog at http://charlieray45.wordpress.com , or his author's Facebook page at http://www.facebook.com/charlieray45.

www.ingramcontent.com/pod-product-compliance
Lightning Source LLC
Chambersburg PA
CBHW070821120626
46556CB00002B/606